WHEN WE CHOOSE TO DIE

by
Kimberly White

Published by Finesse Literary Press

http://www.finesseliterarypress.com

TABLE OF CONTENTS

CHAPTER 1

Time.

It's like a crushing weight of constant wonder. It is also something that many people try to outrun.

But one cannot outrun the inevitable. So why even try? There is no point in trying. There is no point in anything, but that's beside the point. It seems senseless, the way we sit in school every day, wishing the boring hours away and hoping that the clock will tick over faster. Then, when we grow older, we wish the time back; wish for the 'good old days'. As kids, all we want to do is become adults and have responsibilities. But when we get older, all we yearn for is to feel like children again – children with no utility bills or mortgage loans or other everyday worries. I think it is rather funny, ironic actually, that we only want things when they are out of reach, past or present. And we only realise how happy we were at a certain point in time once it is no longer there. Anyway, I'm digressing. The point is that the passing of time is inevitable, so I'm done running.

That is why I am here.

That is why I'm dying.

As I lay on my bed, busy chocking on my own vomit, I am thinking about my life. My meaningless life. When sixty-two potent pills are being processed by one's digestive system, it really makes one think, you know?

The first notion that jumps into my head is: *God, I wasted so much time playing video games.* Then I hastily change my mind. *It was worth it*, I silently tell myself. *So worth it.* All those sleepless nights, playing and squinting at the screen until the birds began to sing at the crack of dawn.

The second notion is of my mom finding me on this bed, looking like this. Nothing but a complete and utter mess. It honestly makes me feel bad, like I've let her and my brother down, but I know they will be fine in the end.

As the months and years go by, they will forget that I even existed and then they'll be able to comfortably carry on with their lives without me. I know some people might think that what I'm doing is incredibly selfish, but it's not. I'm doing my mom and my brother a favour, really.

I abruptly find myself wondering what it is like, death?

No one who is still alive can say whether it's like heaven or hell, whether we will see our deceased loved ones, or whether death is just black. A bottomless, empty, black darkness, like a void in space. Yet, in my mind, there is something quite blissful and rejuvenating about death; the absence of worry, care and obligation.

I also happen to wonder what other people feel in their final moments. Are they happy, sad, angry, regretful?

For me the emotion is simply content. Content that I will never have to be concerned about anything ever again. Content that I don't have to cry myself to sleep anymore. That I don't have to go to school tomorrow. That I'll never have to worry about disappointing my mom ever again.

This is not the reason why I am here, though. This is not the reason why I can now feel the puke clogging up my trachea and spilling over into my burning lungs.

The reason is… well, who cares? I am here and I have just taken my final wheezing breath.

***

The cold, hard surface of the floor is a shock to my body after the soft mattress I was just on, a second ago.

I push myself upright with my elbows and open my hazy eyes to see a plain, endless room, reminiscent of a citadel. The polished marble floors are white, the plastered walls are white and the high ceiling is white. Everything before me is a sharp, blinding white, continuing in every direction imaginable. My immediate surroundings seem so totally desolate, with no furniture or decorations adorning it; nothing that could make this room a place called home.

While I'm considering this barren white space in disbelief, I suddenly hear a lovely, melodious voice behind me.

I turn to see her, a girl whose voice matches her beauty.

Her long, golden-brown hair is flowing down her back and it perfectly frames her heart-shaped face. Her glistening green eyes show her youth more than mine ever could, even though we appear to be around the same age. But there is something else in her eyes other than youth. They also radiate experience in pain, years of experience.

I figure we are the same in a twisted kind of way: two teenagers carrying years of wisdom and pain with them.

'Hi', she says. One simple word, but so entirely calming.

There is sympathy in her tone, not pitiful but in a manner of understanding; a deep understanding of my situation. That alone causes the cold and empty room to feel less deserted and menacing. It's almost comforting.

'Hello, my name is Tom,' I manage to stutter, still stunned by her gorgeous presence.

She is casually dressed in faded blue jeans and a white strappy top, fitting perfectly onto her slender body. Her clothing gives away the fashion trends that were present four or five years ago – simple and informal but elegant. To complement the white cotton top, she is also wearing a sparkling white pearl necklace, matching earrings and a white Alice band. The girl in white…

She giggles shyly before replying, 'I know what your name is.' Then she smiles. A gentle smile that washes a sense of peace over me. She smells like jasmine and fresh lemons.

'What is your name?' I ask with a voice that doesn't sound like my own. The curiosity is eating me up.

'It doesn't matter,' she says, shrugging. 'Not anymore.'

The words hit me like a transport truck. *It doesn't matter*. Nothing does here… I am dead. We are dead.

'What is this place?' I ask suspiciously.

This is not the heaven I've pictured when I was still alive. Neither is it the hell that I've read about in books. In fact, it is the opposite of that. Not that I thought that hell would be engulfed in a sea of flames and managed by red man with horns and a tail, but just not this. I guess everyone's idea of heaven and hell is different. Using this reasoning, I come across yet another irony: some people's idea of hell would be to become separated from their family, while for others that would constitute heaven.

'No one really knows, Tom,' she replies calmly. 'I realise that's not what you want to hear. People always tell me that it is a poor response to a good question. But that is not important. What *is* important is why you are here.'

I stare at her in confusion. What the fuck is that supposed to mean? If she doesn't know what exactly this place is, how come she knows why I am here?

'I like to think of this as the space between,' she tells me. 'You know, the strange universe between life and death... a universe where you get a chance to choose.'

The words frighten me, but I ask the question I know the answer to nonetheless. 'Choose what?'

She smiles once again and I can feel she suspects I already know the answer she's going to give.

'Between continuing to fight and continuing to live on, or die for good. It is that simple, Tom. However, if I ask you to choose right now, I know what your decision will be. That is why I am not going to ask, not yet. Instead, we are going to go forward, together.'

She clasps her tiny hands together in triumph.

CHAPTER 2

'Go forward?' Hell no. I don't want to go forward, that
is the whole fucking point. Why gobble down sixty-two
pills to continue with a future that I'm clearly trying to
avoid? The satire in that is… well, it will suffice to say
that it's just my luck. 'Is this really necessary?' I ask with
a sigh.

She does not respond, merely looks at me expres-
sionless.

I am not worth your time and energy, girl, I think, gazing
back at her. *Just let me die, okay?* Thousands of questions
are swimming around in my mind. Why does she care?
Who is behind this? Does this happen to everyone who
dies? Why do they say yes to living then? Why do they
say yes to dying? I can't do this. I shouldn't have to.

'You are quiet,' the girl in white says, interrupting
my train of thought and thereby ending the uncomfortable silence.

'Well, obviously,' I respond. 'I mean this is so goddamn pointless. Who cares whether I die or not, huh? It

was my decision and mine alone. And it shouldn't be like this.'

'Like what?' she asks, as if no one has ever given her this particular reply to this particularly fucked-up situation.

'This much effort to die, I mean. Life does not carry on forever, you know? No one makes it out alive, so who gives a shit about when it actually happens?'

The harsh statement appears to affect her more than I thought at first. A surge of sadness spreads across her face, as she's staring into nothingness. It's one of those long, endless stares that somehow takes your soul on a journey far away from where you are standing. I know it well, but it is strange seeing it in someone else's eyes.

I guess I've never noticed it in other people's eyes before. We are all so caught up in our own little worlds that we sometimes forget that other human beings also struggle with problems. Even if you tell yourself that you're looking out for others, you only really find out they have issues when they say something, or when it's so obvious from their actions that they might as well scream it in your face. But the human race is not as aware as it likes to pretend. We say we can see a change in behaviour, we say we are there all the time, but you just cannot do that. You cannot constantly support someone else as well as yourself.

'I care,' the girl suddenly says. 'That's why I'm here. I know very little about you, in fact. I know is that your name is Tom and that you are troubled, but I do care.'

I glare at her, not believing any of the words that just came out of her pretty little mouth.

Then, out of the blue, the room begins to change. The walls start revolving and then the place slowly shape-shift into green grass, covered in a thin layer of frost. Different to the smell of nothingness in the white citadel, the aromas of fresh soil and flowers linger in the air. A group of people in formal wear are standing in a semi-circle. I recognise almost all of their sombre faces. That is when I grasp the scene playing out before me – it is my funeral.

The icy cold air makes my cheeks sting and my nose begins to run. I study the group of black-cladded funeral-goers and an eerie feeling of bittersweet nostalgia enters my soul. Seeing my friends and family so sad is genuinely hurtful but, like I said, this was inevitable. It was always going to happen to me: enter the world, live in it, exit the world. All I did was cut out the senseless middle part. They will get over it and move on with their lives. Eventually.

The funeral formalities are about to begin, I notice.

A stranger first reads from a script, then says all the stupid things we say to every person we put in the ground: 'Tom Johnson was such a wonderful person; extremely kind and generous.' I wonder how many people he's read for. How many bodies he's watched getting lowered into a grave.

Who chooses that kind of a job anyway? It is not like you grow up saying, 'Hey! Think how much fun it will be to become a funeral director!' Why? Because you want to dress up dead people, make them look alive and help choose a coffin, that final place where you rot and decay? No way I believe that bullshit. As a kid you want to be an astronaut, a firefighter, a doctor, but not that. People who choose to do that must have a loose screw somewhere.

'He did a lot in his time,' the stranger continues.

I laugh sarcastically. No, I didn't do a lot in my time, mister funeral director. I spent my days and nights playing video games, going to school and doing brainless homework. That doesn't sound like *a lot*. I did nothing in my life that even closely amounts to *a lot*. That's a total fucking lie, generated from a dumb fucking script. The script where we say the same thing about everyone who dies. I bet he gave the exact same speech at a fifty-year-old murderer's burial, the tedious speech he's now spitting out at the suicidal seventeen-year-old boy's funeral.

I watch as an oval teardrop dribbles down my mother's cheek. She is sniffing between her sobs and she's holding my younger brother tightly against her side. I know how devastated she must be. My brother, on the other hand, is not crying at all. He is just staring at the six-foot hole in the ground. The look on his face is familiar, almost as if it were mine. I know he's experiencing that moment when your life is breaking up into pieces around you and there is nothing you can do about it.

Other than my family witnessing the coffin being lowered into the grave my best pal, Jake, is also there, standing on his own, away from the other teenagers – acquaintances from school, many of whom I barely spoke to while I was still alive. My only two other friends, Emma and Rhys, are to Jake's left, shoulder to shoulder under the oak trees.

I'm slightly puzzled as to why Jake is not standing closer to them. The four of us used to do everything together. Now, for some odd reason, Jake is distancing himself from Rhys and Emma. It worries me a little. Perhaps he is taking it worse than the other two. Perhaps he cared more about me than I projected. *Oh well,*

I think to myself, *he will get over it, too. It is not like he's alone in this.*

'How does seeing the people in the vision make you feel?' the girl in white's melodic voice asks me.

'I feel sorry for them,' I reply, 'but the emotions they have, that sadness and pain, it will eventually fade away.' I know I'm right. There is no way she'll disagree with my logic.

'You are wrong,' she says, surprising me. 'This vision is not to make you feel guilty. It is there to show you that you're following the incorrect thought process. You believe no one cares, that they will move on and that your death will have little to no effect on their lives. But you are wrong.' She seems very determined to show me a different side of my ex-life. A life she was never even a part of.

She puts her hands on her hips and says, 'Just because that is *your* perceived reality does not mean it's the *only* reality. For example, a dog's reality is that food is given to it for free and the only reason to go outside is to go for a walk, to exercise those hind legs. And a fish believes that the inside of its bowl is the entire world. There's a term for that, Tom. It's called narrowmindedness.

Okay, I think, *but how is this relevant to me? Are you saying I'm like the fish or the dog?*

The girl in white tightens her jaw, then says, 'Reality isn't consistent, my friend. To you, no one seems to care, but to them, you represented a huge chunk of their daily lives. That is *their* reality. That is *their* perspective.'

I start musing. I've never thought about it like that before. Certainly not right before swallowing those pills.

In the funeral vision, Emma is now speaking quietly as she turns to face Rhys. 'Why did Tom do this to himself?' she asks with moisture filling her large hazel eyes.

'I wish I knew,' Rhys replies. 'I wish I saw the signs earlier. Does that make me a bad friend?'

'It's not your fault,' Emma assures him, patting his arm.

Rhys looks at her tenderly. 'Now that he's not with us any longer, I just wish he knew how much he meant to us.'

I know! Of course I know. I need to tell them that I know. But that is not always enough. I cared about them and they cared about me, but it did not stop the thoughts, the pain and the endless suffering. I could not suffer anymore. I'm glad they didn't know about my inner secrets. I am glad I didn't burden them with all the crap I had going on. This simply proves that I did the right thing. There was no reason for them to know about my agony.

Yes, it was the correct decision to cut my life short. That way Emma and Rhys and Jack were spared from seeing my inevitable downfall. And the worse I would get, the more distant I would have grown from my only friends.

I did not want that for them.

I saved them by ending me.

As if reading my mind, the girl in white says, 'Your friends care, Tom. They have always cared.'

'I know,' I mumble in reply. 'The truth is I cannot complain about them at all. I can't say that they were not there for me, or supportive of my decisions and who I was. I love them and I will always put them before my own interests. Maybe that's the problem… or maybe it is just me.'

'You make it sound like that is a bad thing.'

In the short time that I've known the girl in white, this is the first time I've heard her raise her voice in the slightest.

She must have noticed that she'd startled me, because her tone softens before she says, 'Caring for your loved ones is a good thing, but you have to find a subtle balance between that and making time for yourself. You learn that balance through time and with a lot of patience…' She pauses for a few seconds to allow the concept to sink in. 'You know, Tom, you think you are helping them by not talking about your issues and your negative feelings, but you're not. You are also not helping them by leaving the world with little to no explanation.'

Her words are hurting me on the inside, like long daggers being stabbed into my heart.

'I am not trying to make you feel guilty,' she says, once again as if reading my mind. 'I only want to show you the ripple effect caused by your actions.'

'It does make me feel guilty though,' I tell her, not hurting anymore but feeling angry now. 'What did you expect?'

'I'm not precisely sure,' she says, dropping her head to look at her feet, while biting her lower lip. 'I, uhm, I have never actually done this before.'

'Done what?'

'Showed someone else why it isn't their time to die yet. No one did it for me, that much I can tell you. This doesn't happen to everyone, Tom.'

'So why is it happening to me then?' I ask her impatiently. At least now one of my questions from before has been answered: *Does this happen to everyone who dies? Apparently not.*

'Because I chose you,' she explains. 'I saw you lying there and I had to do something, even though you've chosen to end your life for good. I had to intervene in order for you to make that decision with all the knowledge possible. Then you can be content with your decision, and so can I.'

Her sincere kindness from earlier has returned. I can feel it resonating in the cold air. I bet she was loved while she was alive; dearly loved.

'Okay, so what next then?', I now ask, feeling slightly more willing to continue with 'going forward' as she labelled it earlier. If not for me, at least for her.

'I want you to hear your loved one's speeches,' says the girl in white. 'I want you to hear what those people who really knew Tom Johnson have to say about you.'

CHAPTER 3

The silence is deafening as my mom slowly walks forward to stand in front of the crowd around the grave.

Everyone is staring at her and she's staring back. Her eyes look so bleak and tired. It almost seems like my mother's eyes are more dead than I am. I can feel her nervousness. She is taking shallow breaths and her fingers are tapping against her right thigh. She's never liked public speaking.

'I hope I don't ramble,' she says after composing herself. 'When someone passes away so unexpectedly, you think back to every moment you've shared with them in the past. You think about the small arguments, the trivial discussions and the laughs you've had with them.' Some of the funeral-goers are nodding their heads, while my mother continues. 'I recall the summer when Tom was six years old and I was pretending to be a troll under the playground bridge. He and his friends were the billy goats from the book, and when they tried to cross the bridge I would put on a gruff voice, telling them to get off my precious bridge. They laughed and shrieked while playing their roles as billy goats. I like that memory, because those boys were so carefree and playful. They grew up, though. We all grow up. Then life gets in the way.'

She pauses to look at Rhys and Jake (who played the other two goats) and smiled. 'Anyway,' she resumes, 'he always had a colourful imagination, my Tommy. I think that is why he likes... *liked* video games so much. The visual effects and storylines that those people come up with are simply astounding. I think that would have been the dream job for Tom. Creating new plots and producing characters for video games would have been a perfect fit for my son.'

I guess she thought more about my future than I ever did myself. I have never even considered what I would like to do once I finished school. I had no plans for anything. Expect for dying, of course.

My mom's voice rises a notch. 'Tom was a kind kid, someone who genuinely thought about others and who put their priorities before his own. In hindsight, I now realise that he didn't think about himself as much as he should have. Although I can't bring my son back, I also cannot see someone else do this. So if anyone ever feels like they are not worthy, or tired of life, come talk to me. I am always here and even if I am a stranger to some of you, it does not mean we can't become friends.

We need to support each other if we want to prevent a similar tragedy. We can't have another Tom in this community.'

The tears well up in my eyes. I'm too ashamed to blink and reveal my sorrow to the girl in white. But she is focused on my mom, I observe, consumed by the moving speech.

My mother concludes with: 'I miss him every day and every hour, and I will never get to tell him that. I'll never be able to explain to him how much I loved him. I can also never tell him about the complete shock and grief when I saw his body with the note on his chest. The note that contained only one word: Goodbye. And now I have to say that word. So, goodbye my dearest Tom... Goodbye only in body, not in spirit, as that part of you will stay with us in our memories. We will keep you alive in the footprints you left in our hearts. Finally, today, but not for the last time, I must tell you: I love you, my son.'

'I knew my mom would be the one to find me,' I say to the girl in white. I can feel how my vocal cords are trembling.

'She didn't, your brother did.'

'What?' I reply in disbelief.

'He came into your room asking for help with his math homework. He then called your mom who phoned 911.'

That is not what I wanted. Not by a long shot.

The thought of him seeing me dead like that, with puke running down my chin and my eyes glazed over is not only upsetting, it's appalling. He will never get over such a horrific sight. It's going to scar him for life.

I sit down for a minute, flattening the frozen grass leaves under my scrawny buttocks.

'I want you to know you cannot take that back,' says the girl in white, approaching and sitting down beside me. Her voice turns more serious. 'Even if you choose to live, that memory will always stay with your brother.'

'Alright, but I can still be there for him after he saw that?' I say without thinking.

'Of course you can,' she replies, now sounding friendlier. 'Brothers must stick together and family members must support each other. If they don't, they aren't family.'

I look at my friends and family around the grave and come to the conclusion that she is right. We always stick by each other, no matter what the circumstances. Whether it is a case of feeling under the weather, or breaking up with a girlfriend, or a pet dying, we always support one another. That is what a family is supposed to do – protect each other from the cruel, harsh world out there.

CHAPTER 4

Jake now approaches the front of the crowd to take my mother's place. His hands are shaking and the hem of his long coat is brushing against the grass. When he reaches the spot where my mom stood a moment ago, he looks up at the dozens of eyes waiting for him to mutter his first words. He glances at Emma and relaxes a little.

Then he begins to speak, reading from a thin stack of cue cards in his gloved hands. 'Tom was my best friend, but one can never know all of another person's thoughts or secrets. I have one of those secrets too. What Tom did not know – and I'm sure neither does any of you present – is that I also once attempted to take my own life.'

Gasps are coming from the funeral-goers, especially my mom and Jake's mom. I'm glad I am sitting down because this news rips through me like a chainsaw through the trunk of a pine tree. I don't only have moist eyes anymore, I'm sobbing like a baby. This is all too much to process. The girl in white puts her arm around my waist in support.

With a wave of her other arm she somehow pauses the funeral vision and says, 'Take a moment, Tom. Let out the pain and breathe deeply. You can do it. You have no idea how strong you are. Remember, you have been fighting your whole life, that is why you are this resilient.'

We sit there for a while, contemplating.

'Okay, I'm ready,' I tell her a few minutes later, although I'm still trying to get full control over my emotions.

'Are you sure?' she asks. Her voice is oozing with sincere sympathy.

'Yes, I want to hear Jake's speech. I *need* to hear it.'

After another wave of the girl in white's arm, Jake's voice resumes in the vision. 'But the major difference between me and Tom is that I survived. I woke up the day after my suicide attempt like nothing happened. I continued with my daily routine, the same as I've always done.' Jake stops to look down at the cards, then continues. 'If I could swop places with him, I would. Tom was a much better person than I am, and I should have noticed the signs. But I didn't and neither did any of you. You cannot stand here today and say how you knew him and how you cared for him when you never gave a rat's ass while he was still alive. Stop preaching about change in behaviour when a person dies and do something when they are alive.'

I can see how the anger is rising in my best friend's soul, until it explodes through his eyes. With flaring nostrils and a flushed face, he shouts, 'Do not pretend like you care now! You should have cared a month ago, a year ago.'

I get up, jump into the vision and hug him. I know Jake cannot feel me and that he doesn't even know I am there with him, but it's the best I can do, given my dire situation.

He breaks down in tears as people are gawking at him with wide eyes. His mom is trying to pull him away, but he remains motionless. 'I am not done!' he snarls. 'I loved that young man, and I hope that no one as good as him will ever feel the need to end it all.' Jake all of a sudden tilts his head upwards to face the sky. 'Tom, if you can hear me,' he cries, 'I cared! We all cared and I'm sorry if you thought you couldn't come to us for help. Because I would much rather you came to me than me making this speech today, embarrassing myself in front of everyone.'

I laugh silently. 'Well, you *can* be quite an embarrassing guy,' I whisper to myself, recalling an incident where he threw a peanut butter sandwich at a teacher in class and blamed me for it afterwards.

In the end, I got into detention and had to do a walk of shame in front of the entire class. It was not funny at the time but now I somehow find it hilarious. The way that sandwich headed straight towards Mrs Ellory's permed hair – seemingly in slow motion – and the way she yelled as the sandwich flipped open at point ninety-nine, causing the two sticky slices to slam into her curls. Her eyes bulged out in pure fury, but her being only four-foot-ten made her look like the least intimidating person in the school, and that was including the eighth graders.

Thinking about memories like that reminds me of the good moments in life. It's really something that's been amiss before I killed myself. When you're feeling so low about life in general, it is hard to think of happy times in your past. The sadness consumes your every day, making all the good recollections blurry, until your whole life is like a stranger to you. The faces you once knew then become equivalent to people you briefly walk past on the street, and you feel like you cannot talk to them anymore. You can't explain all your issues and worries to random faces, and *that's* what makes you feel so alone.

But now that I'm dead I can finally take a step back and look at my seventeen years on earth to realise that I was perhaps not as alone as I felt all the time.

CHAPTER 5

'Do I have to choose now?' I hear myself ask. There is a hint of concern in my voice.

'Not yet. I want to take you forward a bit further. I know you won't want to see it, but I need you to understand the good and the bad aspects of your future. That is life, Tom.' The girl in white smiles peacefully at me. 'You need the bad moments in order to experience and appreciate the good ones. That is why I want to show you the happiness you could encounter as well as the sadness. You will soon learn how you can overcome those dreadful times, to end up stronger than you were before.'

'But if I choose to live then I will know everything anyway.'

'Life has many outcomes, Tom. The scenario I'm going to present to you is just one of them. It doesn't mean that it embodies your exact future. However, it will show you what may come of living a full life.'

'So, it could end up worse than what I'm about see,' I snap at her, instantly regretting my tone. I lower my voice, then add, 'And I could have a miserable life ahead of me.'

She appears not be fazed by my outburst. 'Or it could be so much better. You have to remember something: a negative outlook on life helps no one, especially not you.'

I sigh in frustration but deep down I know that she's right.

I have always looked at the world in a bad light, only seeing the sorrow and suffering in it. Animals becoming extinct, homeless people freezing in the cold, corrupt businesses causing ruined economies... Which makes me think: How can anyone possibly be a billionaire? I've never understood how you could make that much money.

But there are good things in the world too. Like devoted people helping to save the environment, old-age homes, loving families who care for each other, charities and aid organisations. People are trying, and that is what I should focus on. It's just that it can be so damn hard when all the negative things are in your face all day long, in the news and on social media. It is difficult to look past the fact that Mother Earth is slowly dying, even if there are people out there trying to help and to stop the madness.

'Okay, I'll give you the benefit of the doubt,' I say with a grin on my face. 'Let's do this before I change my mind,'

She smiles back and waves her arm.

The scenery in the vision begins to change once more, spinning around us like a giant kaleidoscope. The funeral images disappear, then the frosted grass and the cold air evolves into a pleasantly warm day. The sun is beaming onto my face and that's when I hear a familiar laugh.

'Emma!' I say excitedly.

Gazing at my friend in the new vision, I see that she is busy loading a bulky suitcase into the trunk of a car.

'Why is your shit always taking up most of the room, Emma girl?' Rhys asks jokingly.

'Purely to annoy you,' she says with a smirk. 'You don't need the space anyway, Rhys. I mean, you own a total of three t-shirts, two baseball caps and one pair of jeans.'

'Ha,' Rhys responds. 'There are better things to spend your money on than clothes. There is more to life than tangible possessions, you know? Anyway, just because you have a lot of clothes it doesn't mean you have style.'

I know Emma isn't someone who'll let him get away with taking the piss out of her.

She snorts, then says, 'That's rich coming from someone with an Ellen DeGeneres haircut.'

Another laugh comes from behind and Jake approaches the car in the street. 'She's not entirely wrong, dude,' he chips in. 'I mean, what is it with that haircut?'

I'm happy to see that his spirits are high again.

Rhys has no response other than a sheepish look on his face. He climbs into the backseat of the car. The thing is, he is wrong about Emma. I know she has amazing style. She usually wears miniskirts with tights and black shoes or ankle boots, and her makeup is always carefully applied. Her eyeliner is perfectly winged (which complements her cute little nose) and the dark eyeshadow makes her blue eyes look like the clearest water you have ever seen. Her hair is dyed raven black, with green streaks underneath, so when she tucks it behind her pointy ears the green streaks show, making her sexy in a pixie kind of way.

During my years in high school, everyone always wanted to date Emma. Not only because of her looks but because of her compassionate personality.

She has only officially dated two people up to now.

The first one was a tall guy who was mean and controlling. Their relationship barely lasted four weeks before she dumped him because he was cheating on her. Ironically, the second person she dated was the girl he cheated on her with. They got along very well but Emma's girlfriend moved away to Texas a couple of months later. Sadly, they weren't able to make the long-distance thing work.

But here she is now, laughing with her friends, our friends, and then Jake wraps his arms around her and kisses her lovingly on the top of her head.

They might be dating, I think to myself.

That actually makes a lot of sense. Their personalities are so similar it's almost impossible to miss.

CHAPTER 6

Jake and Emma also climbs into the car and the three of them drive off, with Jake behind the wheel.

The vision jumps a few of hours into the future, until the car stops in Harrisburg, Pennsylvania. It's evening now.

Emma flings herself out the passenger door and stretches her legs and arms. The beautiful city, sitting alongside the mighty Susquehanna River, is buzzing with people rushing to their respective destinations; some in cars, some on bicycles or motorcycles, but most of them on foot.

'A road trip to a big city sounds like a lot of fun,' the girl in white tells me, dimples forming on her rosy cheeks.

'Yeah,' I agree. 'I've always loved travelling from one place to another, taking in the scenery.' Then I stare at her for a short while. The city lights are creating a silvery halo around her head as she flicks her hair back to get a better look at the concrete jungle around us.

It reminds me of our position. We are not really here, we are dead. That is when I comprehend that even if I choose to live, she will still be stuck here. This gorgeous girl with all the potential in the world will never get a chance to go on another road trip or fall in love and get married.

The thought saddens me. However, her touch brings me back to the moment. I put a fake smile on my face and she looks at me with concern in her bright eyes.

'Are you okay, Tom?' she asks in a tender voice.

I only nod, knowing that if I speak now she will hear my voice crack.

'Alright, but it's fine if you're not. You don't have to be happy all the time, you know?'

She always seems to know what to say. I think it's because we are so similar in some ways. I also like to believe that she is sort of making certain statements to herself, as if it's what she needs to hear as well. *You don't have to be happy all the time…*

The sound of Jake's voice returns my eyes to the vision.

'Tom would have loved this,' he says to Rhys. 'Spending a summer in the city is something he always talked about. He probably would have done it sooner if he just stopped playing those silly video games.' He chuckles. 'The dude most likely didn't see sunlight for days at one point.'

'Well,' Rhys replies, 'tomorrow we can see it for him.'

I can tell that this is hurting Jake. He is also showing signs of that fury at the funeral earlier. 'We shouldn't have to,' he says, raising his voice. 'He should be here with us, and screw him for not.' He turns his head to hide his face from Emma and Rhys. 'I'm sorry guys, it's just–'

'We get it, Jake,' Emma interjects. 'Honestly, we all think the same. We all wish he was here.'

Rhys nods in agreement.

Jake slowly turns to face them again and blinks his eyes. 'So, what should we go see first?' he asks, attempting to change the subject and the mood.

'I would love to visit the state museum,' Emma says in pure excitement. Her love and knowledge of history have always astonished me.

'The museum it is then,' says Jake, putting a strong arm around her shoulders.

CHAPTER 7

The vision skips to a couple of months later and the new location is now my former school grounds.

Some students are hurrying through the hallways to get to their classes on the other side of the school in time. Other pupils – those without a care in the world – are merely strolling along without worrying whether they'll make it to their next lessons or not.

I'm grateful that I don't have to deal with it all at this point. Having to put up with all those people I couldn't stand. Faking it throughout the day until I could go home, put on my earphones and lose myself in my games. My *fictional* games. Because reality is so fucking overrated.

The bell rings and my classmates sit down to learn the most useless shit in the world. Jake is seated next to Rhys. About fifteen minutes into the lesson the teacher gets called to the principal's office and, as soon as she's left, a student at the back of the class starts talking about my funeral. More specifically, about Jake's outburst.

'He always thinks he's better than everyone else and that's the reason I'm not surprised by what he did. But still. Imagine yelling at someone's family during a funeral? How pathetic is that? A lack of manliness if you ask me.'

The girl in white frowns at the bully. 'Toxic masculinity,' she says, shaking her head.

'Typical for guys like that,' I reply sourly. 'I reckon he's just overcompensating for a lack of something else.'

We both laugh and then she continues to talk about him.

'He is desperate,' she says. 'Desperate for the girls to think that he's macho. Desperate for his friends to laugh with him, for their attention. I hope he can someday get over the idea that he needs reassurance from others, but I guess that is what school can do to you. You are hurled into a sea of other people and you become invisible. You become nothing. And I guess everyone deals with that in their own different ways. It is just a shame that he feels the need to bring down other people to feel superior.'

I sense an urge to find out more about her. 'Were you ever bullied?' I ask. 'Is that why you are here?'

She brushes off my question by saying, 'Like I've told you before: It does not matter anymore.'

In the vision, Jake is now turning red in the face as the bully resumes: 'And then you're crying like that in front of everyone. That's so fucking pitiful man. I don't know how the hell you got a girl like Emma. You're such a baby.'

The bully's so-called friends are practically howling with laughter when he says, 'You know what, Jake? If I was your best mate, I would off myself too.'

'That's going too far,' the girl in white hisses in a rage.

Moments after she uttered that, Jake stands up and turns to the boys in the back of the classroom. 'How dare you speak about Tom like that?' he says in a thundering voice. 'You are a nobody and you have no bloody right to talk about anyone looking the way you do, fatso. The way you sit there, breathing through your ugly mouth and looking like a mixture between Shrek and Jabba the Hut's child.'

I can't help but laugh at that one, even though I know the situation is about to turn very messy.

Rhys rises to his feet, then takes Jake by the arm and walks him out, whilst Jake is shouting, 'It should have been you, you worthless piece of scum!'

I gasp at hearing Jake say something so hateful. He is usually such a peaceful lad. Now I've seen two outbursts. One at my funeral and another one right in the middle of the classroom. 'Did I do that to him?' I ask the girl in white.

'Do not say that,' she warns me. 'Do not blame yourself. Anger is a rather important emotion during the grieving process. And Jake is still grieving, believe me. But we will talk about that later. Let's watch your friends for now.'

Rhys and Jake walks into the men's restroom, both of them with sweat stains on the back of their shirts.

'That was a little harsh, Jake,' Rhys says in a concerned but relatively quiet tone.

'I know, sorry. I didn't mean it, it just came out.'

'I understand,' says Rhys. 'But you're going to get yourself expelled, and Tom would be calling you a complete dipshit for letting that moron get you expelled or suspended.'

Rhys has always been so level-headed, even in the most stressful circumstances. 'You have to ignore him,' he now tells Jake. 'I know it's hard and quite frankly not fair but be the better person. Rise above it, buddy.'

'Alright, alright,' Jake replies, raising his hands to his shoulders in surrender.

CHAPTER 8

I sit down on the dirty linoleum floor of the classroom just as Rhys and Jake re-enters the scene. The girl in white sits down silently beside me, holding my hand.

'I wish I could take away their heartache,' I tell her. I'm close to tears again, but this time I manage to stay strong.

'I understand that more than you know,' she replies. Then she closes her eyes and inhales air through her nose.

I don't think she wants me to see her pain. We are similar that way, not willing to discuss our issues with others.

'It is not always like this for them,' she now says, opening her crystal clear eyes. 'Of course you will always be in their minds, but they do experience happiness as well. Look, I don't want you to feel like you must go back because their happiness is dependent on you being there. If you choose to live, you must do so because you want to experience *everything* with them.'

She analyses my facial expression for a response, so I ask, 'Why are you showing me all these events?'

'I first wanted to show you how much they care about you and then, once you noticed they were also happy, you wouldn't reason that your death did not impact them. Basically, I am trying for you to grasp how you influenced your friends. But the reason to choose life should not be to go back for them, as a kind of obligation. It should be because life is better than you think. To go back must be to see how you and your loved ones grow in strength.'

This is clearly her first time doing anything like this, since she was rambling a little when she spoke. But it makes sense all the same, and she is only trying to help me out. I know she doesn't want me to feel guilty for leaving this 'space between'. She's only teaching me the importance of existence. However, even though I want to see life as this awesome concept, I can't. It's too difficult. I cannot see past the repetitive pattern of wake-up, go-to-school, return-home, go-to-sleep. It is boring and draining, and it begs the question: 'Shouldn't there be more to life?'

***

The hard floor gradually turns soft and we are now sitting on a plush woven carpet. I see a room with walls covered in posters of music artists and album covers, ranging from pop to rock to heavy metal.

I've been here before. It's Emma's room.

She is crazy about all kinds of music and movies, enjoying films from musicals like Mama Mia to horror movies like The Conjuring. Her and Jake are sitting on her bed, eating pasta. Emma is really wolfing down the macaroni, as if she's in a rush to go somewhere, whereas Jake is picking at the food like a bird. In-between eating, they are talking about school and Jake's new part-time job at the local supermarket. Basic stuff, but they appear to be content.

***

Over the past half hour, I've watched scenes where they went on dates and hung out with other friends. They argued over Emma getting hit on by other guys and made up afterwards. They played chess, watched television and cooked together. And by cook I mean sticking a frozen pizza into the oven and waiting for it to be heated.

Jake brought her a pet frog, which Emma hated at first, thinking it was gross and not something that should be a pet, but she ultimately grew to love the little guy. She built a bigger bamboo cage and gave the frog some insects and other weird stuff she said it would like.

'You love that thing more than you love me,' Jake joked.

'Well he is cuter than you,' she jested back.

'Oh, really,' Jake said, widening his eyes. He picked her up and threw her on the bed and she laughed. He pinned her down and banged on the bedpost with his palm, saying, 'One, two, three and you are out!' She pushed him off whilst giggling and calling him names. That was how their relationship worked – they ribbed each other.

'You need a haircut, handsome,' she said, ruffling his hair. Then she gently slapped him across the head. 'And that is for tackling me,' she added with a grin so wide it exposed nearly all of her perfectly white teeth.

Their relationship grew serious over time and became this beautiful thing. I did not even get to see all of it, just some glimpses through the girl in white's projected vision. I was not a part of it, or there for them when they were angry or sad as their relationship evolved.

I'm beginning to lean towards a choice where I want to see it all. But not from here.

I want to see my friends in real life.

CHAPTER 9

'Tom, do you happen know what the five stages of grief are?' the girl in white asks, raising her eyebrows.

'Yes, sure. Denial, anger, bargaining, depression and then acceptance. I have never experienced any of it though.'

She looks at me seriously. 'You are about to see it.'

'Those stages do not last forever,' I tell her. 'Is it really worth it to see a month or two of my friends and family's sad lives when I can see them happy and thriving?'

The girl in white appears to be perplexed as she says, 'It never fully goes away, the grief. Of course it gets easier but it never completely disappears. And don't worry, you will get to see the good parts of their lives too. As I've said before, I want you to witness both sides of the coin.'

The scene shifts again, to another place that I am familiar with – the cosy living room in my mom's house. A tree is perfectly placed in the corner of the room, not too far from the fireplace but far enough not be a potential burn-the-house-down risk. The glitzy Christmas decorations are arranged in an OCD fashion, with even the tree branches being somewhat symmetrical. Dozens of bright Christmas lights are illuminating the entire living room, sparkling and shimmering in the evening air.

The whole setting brings up memories such as dancing with your best friend in an empty street, or when you're a toddler and your dad swings you around in circles, holding on to your ankles. Or when you laugh so hard that your stomach hurts, but it's that good kind of pain where you have tears running down your cheeks, all because of one funny joke. It brings out those tiny but flawless memories of joy that you cherish until the moment you close your eyes forever.

I notice that the red and green baubles are also positioned in the same order on the Christmas tree: red, red, green, red, red, green. Underneath the tree is a collection of organised gifts, each in the best place for its particular size and shape. Traditional but rather classy woollen stockings are hanging against the beige wall beside the fireplace, with the exact distance between each stocking. One of them is overflowing with carefully picked gifts; DVDs, CDs, mints and chocolate. The fireplace combined with the stockings on the wall and the Christmas tree in the corner give the impression of a photo belonging on the front page of a glossy magazine. In addition, the stark contrast of the white-washed wooden floor makes everything appear even more vivid and striking.

I turn to examine the rest of the room. The bay windows are painted white around the rims, to mimic frost on the inside. It reminds me of the times before triple glazing and when the milk man still came to deliver milk to your front door every morning. Above the windows are posters of reindeer and elves dashing through the snow.

The smell of baked turkey, gravy and potatoes is drifting in from the direction of the kitchen, lifting one's mood by meeting the nose with a soft hello. A home-cooked meal almost without fail smells better than a takeaway burger or a restaurant dish. It brings with it nostalgia, I reckon.

'My mother is always so meticulous about the Christmas dinner table,' I say to the girl in white.

She smiles from ear to ear. 'It's incredibly beautiful. The colour scheme and the way it is all laid out. Stunning.'

She is right. The cherry-red table cloth and the shiny gold runner down the middle, together with the gold-edged white serviettes, folded to perfection, makes for quite a spectacular sight. A tall brass candelabra, containing six burning candles, complete the pretty picture.

Which leads my eyes to something else – the number of porcelain dinner plates. She set an extra one by mistake. It must have been habit or maybe my mom's wishful thinking that I would walk down those stairs at any moment, like I've done on so many occasions before.

'Denial,' the girl in white now says. 'A stage people tend to stay in for the longest. Perhaps it is easier to pretend that all is okay than to face the truth.' She sounds so much like me, her thought process must be creepily similar.

The food is all laid out and ready to be consumed within thirty minutes. It has always fascinated me how food dishes that are prepared during several hours of cooking can disappear so quickly.

Although, I have to say, in our house the time difference between preparing food and consuming it has never been a problem. I've watched my mom host Christmas dinners for the whole family plenty of times before. Standing in the kitchen all afternoon is not hard work for her at all. She always thoroughly enjoys it. I think it's due to that satisfactory feeling when everyone says how full they are from not being able to stop eating her delicious cuisine.

I watch as my brother attempts to pull a Christmas cracker with our grandad, who on a normal day would only sit in a slump, watching television and smoking his pipe. He is usually a stereotypical, grumpy grandad but not today. Today he wears a smile and then a lets out a chuckle under his breath because the cracker is beating my brother in strength. He is unable to tear it open at his end, in order to win the cheap, plastic prize inside.

'You would not survive the war, boy,' my grandad jokes. He rarely made jokes or even interacted with us before. So, to see him like this is strange but also wonderful. Maybe it was just me. Perhaps that's why he was never friendly when I was still around. Maybe I was the problem.

After a swift dinner prayer by my grandad, everyone digs in, dishing up chunks of food onto their plates. The spread is marvellous: sliced turkey, colourful roasted vegetables, baked potatoes and many other delicacies. I stare at the pigs in blankets – you know, those succulent sausages wrapped in strips of bacon – my absolute favourite part of a Christmas dinner. My mouth is watering. It's almost as if I can taste the salty flavour just by the sight of them.

'It looks and smells divine,' the girl in white says.

'Yeah, nothing better than mom's home-cooked food.' Suddenly, all all the joyful recollections of family get-togethers come rushing into my mind. That is the thing about being sad: all the good memories are suppressed, engulfed by your miserable emotions, until that is the only thing you can remember. That's why it is always a battle within. You are constantly fighting your own thoughts.

'I forgot how much I loved this holiday and the festivities surrounding it,' I now say. 'It feels like all the memories got stolen from me somewhere along the line.'

'I understand that,' the girl in white replies in a comforting tone. 'Sometimes it's like... how do I put this? It's like your good memories become a type of virus and then your own body attacks them, unknowingly causing you harm.'

She was stuttering throughout the statement and it may not have been poetic, but it's by far the best explanation I've ever heard for describing my misery. I love how she is so understanding of everything I'm going through and I adore that relaxing feeling radiating from her face.

My brother passes a gift to my mom. It is poorly wrapped, with Sellotape sticking up and folded over each portion where the gluey side was pressed together by mistake. The wrapping paper is faded and slightly torn in places. She smiles politely and thanks him, taking the gift with her well-manicured hands.

As she unravels the wrapping, Andre waits impatiently. The unwrapped paper reveals a circular photo frame, painted white and decorated with baby-blue diamond patterns. Inside the frame is a photograph of me dressed up as Wonder Woman, her being my favourite superhero.

I was bullied a lot for that costume in my kindergarten years, but the photo now makes me snicker, thinking about how Emma dressed up as Ironman and Jake as Aquaman. That Halloween we received the most candy ever and I adored that Wonder Woman outfit, especially the gold headband. My mom spent hours making it and I really enjoyed that Halloween, save for the bullying and the candy-induced stomach ache the next day of course.

It was one of those days when my mom became my hero and I was particularly proud to be her son. She was able to make a costume that I loved from nothing but a picture and her creativity completely mesmerised me.

The girl in white chuckles upon seeing the photo. 'I love that, it's so original,' she says with a huge grin on her face, one that matches mine in the picture.

'Thanks.' I can feel myself blushing but I involuntarily add, 'I looked sexy there, don't you think?'

Her chuckle transforms into a laugh. 'For sure. You're a stunning Wonder Woman. If we lived in the same area at the same time, I think we would have been good friends.'

The smile on my face is starting to hurt my cheeks. This girl truly knows how to cause joy in my heart. She is capable of turning a happy moment into an ecstatic one. At least for me, that is.

In the vision, my mother thanks my brother Andre for the thoughtful gift, overwhelming him with a tight hug.

Everyone else is now also opening their gifts. Halfway through, I see my mom walk out of the room. I follow her to the hallway, where I watch her gripping the photo frame whilst crying softly.

'I don't think she will ever fully get over your death,' the girl in white says. 'But it will get a little simpler over the years. There will always be times which will remind her more of you, and this is one of them.'

I think about my mother's memories. She is probably now recalling that Halloween (when I was a boy of only five) reminiscing on when I received my first bike the week after. I was yelling at her not to let go as my feet worked the pedals, being restricted by the wind up the slope, still too small and weak to go fast against the gradient.

My grandad walks into the hallway and I roll my eyes because I don't want him to interrupt my mother's sweet memories. This is no time for his 'man-up' speech, which I'm so sure he's about to give.

'Tom was a goofy kid, alright,' he says in his raspy voice.

The words take me by surprise. I didn't even realise he knew my name, let alone thought of me as a little rascal.

'I miss him,' he adds, 'and I regret not speaking to him more often. I guess…' Then my grandpa stops talking for a moment, most likely thinking and planning what he is going to say next. 'I guess I should have tried harder, but I always feel so disconnected with their generation. All they do is talk about video games or watch video clips on their phones. How am I supposed to relate to that?'

He doesn't sound angry. He sounds more frustrated with himself because he cannot associate with us teenagers.

'I am trying now, with Andre,' he continues. 'I want to be a part of my grandchild's life.'

My mother gives him half a smile and pats his shoulder. 'That's good, Dad,' is all she says.

'Are you ready to go back to the others?' my grandad asks.

'Yes, I think I am,' my mom answers. She puts the framed photograph down on the rosewood dresser in front of her and then follows her father back into the living room.

'I like your grandad,' the girl in white says to me.

'He is not usually like that and I've never really bonded with him,' I admit. 'But if my death makes him a better person, then I'm glad for my family. My mother needs a caring and supportive dad.'

I'm feeling much more at ease now that I've been assured that my brother and my mom are not alone.

'You know you can change that relationship in real life, right?' the girl in white says, pointing at my grandfather where he is now kneeling beside the Christmas tree. 'You've heard how he feels and all you have to do is talk to him. You will probably find he is as lonely as you.'

'Who says I am lonely?' I ask abruptly,

She remains calm as she responds with, 'It's just a feeling I get, you know? Call it female intuition if you like.'

CHAPTER 10

Life on repeat.

That has always been one of my biggest fears.

While I was still alive, my mom would get up at 7 a.m. every morning. Then she'd shower, get dressed, brush her teeth, put on her makeup, make her morning coffee, go to work and sit at a desk from 8 a.m. to 5 p.m. Thereafter she would go home, eat dinner, watch TV and go to bed. Wash, rinse, repeat. It was almost as if her body was on autopilot, that's how instinctual the routine was.

This routine hasn't changed much since my death, I now learn. I'm watching the girl in white's projected vision as it shifts to my mom's office. She is tastefully dressed in a cream blouse under a black suede jacket, navy slacks and black high heels. She looks up from her desk and notices two of her co-workers staring at her with menacing eyes. They are both wearing nametags: Fred Powell and Roger Anderson. When they realise my mom has seen them stare, they look back at each other and begin to whisper – glancing at her every now and again – like high school girls gossiping about who's hairdo is worse or which boy they kissed at the dance on Saturday. Some people never grow up. Another sad reality in life.

I catch some words and phrases of the things they are whispering. '…her son…' '…been four months…' '…looks totally exhausted…'

My mom is trying to ignore them, I observe. But then she hears something she cannot ignore any longer. It's one of those sentences that pierces like a bullet.

'Committing suicide is goddamn selfish,' the colleague named Fred says, glaring at my mom like a falcon.

Her head slowly rises above her computer screen and she gives Fred a look I have never seen before; a look of pure peril and wrath. Her usually kind face quickly contorts into a grimace that even the devil will fear. I don't know if my ears are deceiving me, but I can actually hear her growl, like a dog defending its territory.

Freddy takes a step back, realising the mistake he's made. A terrible mistake that would teach him a lesson he should have been taught when he was five years old. The lesson that educates you on how your words affect other people, especially if you start to make it personal.

My mother walks up to him with a certain intent of attack in her stride. I want to stop her, to tell her that it's not worth it, but I am dead. I cannot help her anymore, so all I will have to do is watch her punch this asshole and then get fired. However, when she reaches the man, she does not raise her fist. She speaks to him instead.

'Do you know what it's like to fight with yourself?' she asks rhetorically. 'You have to struggle with every breath you take. Every second and minute that goes by, you have to fight to keep pushing forward. When that becomes your daily life, it is not selfish to commit suicide, it's a way of finally giving yourself relief. Relief from the bitter pain and suffering you're enduring, and relief from the fact that you won't have to fight each breath anymore.'

Fred's eyes are vacant and that makes it difficult to figure out what he is thinking right now. His buddy, Roger, has backed away in an attempt to escape the war scene he was undoubtedly expecting.

'When you take your own life, you are only passing that struggle and pain on to your loved ones,' Fred finally says. His demeanour is calm and collected, as if he can see the pain in my mother's eyes but he's ignoring it.

She looks at him in disdain while saying, 'Freddy, imagine someone is in so much agony that they feel death is the only rational answer. In such a harsh reality, despite their actions causing pain to their loved ones, they realise it's the only way out of the self-conflict they are facing every day. Have you even thought about that?'

He laughs at her. 'That's just dumb logic, Lucy,' he says, then picks up his mug of coffee and walks away.

My mom appears to be rather gobsmacked. She is simply standing there in silence, motionless, seemingly replaying the unsettling conversation over in her head.

One of the young interns approaches her and asks if she is okay. He's a sweet guy who attended my school a few years back. Gabe is his name, if I recall correctly. I was always jealous of his dark complexion and his curly black hair. He would come to school every day looking smart and organised, while yours truly looked like I'd stuck my head out of the bus window.

My mother doesn't hear him at first, so he repeats, in the most caring tone he can muster, 'Ma'am, are you okay?'

'Oh yes, thank you,' replies my mom. It's the exact same response she gives to everyone whenever the subject of my suicide comes up.

She wanders back to her workstation, sits down behind the desk and then gazes at the computer screen. It is now quiet in the office, barring the sound of machinery – air conditioning units, a printer, a coffee grinder, and the low buzzing of computers, including the tower case under my mom's desk. The humming of the disc drive, processor, fan and wires that are creating the colours on her screen.

What happens next can only be described as a frenzy.

My mother picks up the mouse and hurls it at the screen, causing the little navigating device to shatter into pieces. Next in line is the keyboard, which is repeatedly smashed against the corner of the steel desk, keys and tiny springs flying everywhere. Finally, she pulls the screen out of its docking station, flings it to the floor and then slumps down beside its cracked remains, weeping uncontrollably.

Gabe comes running back to help her up before hugging her. It' a nice gesture, but I have a strong hunch that the only hug she genuinely wants at this moment is from the one person who can't give it to her.

CHAPTER 11

The tick-tock of the clock against the wall is the only sound in the room as my mom's boss sits in front of her with a sorrowful expression on his face. It feels like hours before he speaks and the suspense is killing me. What is going to happen? Will he fire her? Suspend her?

He finally opens his mouth. 'They deserve to be punished. I will not tolerate Roger and Freddy's behaviour and I cannot believe either of them had the audacity to speak to you like that. But I really wish you came to me when you felt angry, Lucy, rather than smashing the company assets to smithereens. He lets out a long sigh, most likely in preparation for his next statement.

'If you are going to fire me, just do it already,' my mother says with tight lips. Her voice is trembling.

'I am not going to lay you off, although the amount of paperwork you are making me do almost warrants it,' he jokes, in a weak attempt to lighten the mood. 'You are going to take some time off… Don't look at me like that, It's non-negotiable. Once you feel better, you'll undergo a psychological evaluation to see if you are fit to return.'

'That's just great,' my mom says sarcastically.

'This is not a punishment Lucy, it is me looking out for you. You will thank me later, believe me. And it's paid leave, so you don't have to worry about your financial well-being during your recovery. Just focus on yourself and your remaining son. He needs you right now.'

I met her boss at a work function where Rhys and I were waiters and I instantly liked him. He came across as very understanding and sympathetic towards his employees.

My mother eventually nods in agreement. I think she understands that there is nothing else she can do.

After a quick 'Thank you, sir,' she leaves his offices and makes it outside into the crisp early afternoon air.

She takes her time walking home because I know her home doesn't feel like a home anymore now that I'm gone. It feels like a plain old house; a roof over her head; a place where she can eat and sleep.

***

When my mom arrives at the house twenty minutes later, she enters the living room where Andre is lounging on one of the leather couches, listening to music on his phone, like he usually does after school.

He takes out one of his earbuds to ask, 'What are you doing home so early, Mom?'

Instead of replying, she just stares bluntly at him for a moment, then shuffles into the kitchen. Her movements are zombie-like, as if she were sleep walking. I am not even sure that she heard my brother speak.

The girl in white, who is never really fazed about anything, looks pretty concerned as well. Her calm nature is now superseded by a kind of surrogate anxiety.

My mom pauses at the kitchen window and glares into the dishwashing basin. Water from the tap is dripping onto a plate with a knife on it – two items to wash up.

Andre sneaks up behind her and says, 'Mom?'

'Why do I always have to clean up after you?' she scolds him. 'You are fifteen bloody years old and you cannot even wash your own dishes! Pathetic.'

'Fine, I will clean it now!' Andre snaps. 'Although I don't see the big deal. It's only one fucking plate.'

'Yeah, a plate here, a mug there, they all add up, Andre. You never clean up behind yourself and I always have to beg you to help tidying the house. Why do I have to do everything around here, you lazy snot?'

'For fuck's sake, Mom, if I am so much of a problem I will leave then. I don't need you, I can live at Charlie's. In fact, his parents will welcome me with open arms.'

My brother has tears in his eyes and I can see that they are both at a breaking point. Which is to be expected if you are talking about moving out in the wake of arguing over a stupid porcelain dinner plate.

Andre storms off to his room, exclaiming how he is going to 'pack a bag and get the hell outta here.' My mother is left speechless for the second time in one hour. She slowly sits down at the kitchen table and put her head in her hands, sniffing and sobbing like a child. All I want to do is hug her, but all I can do is watch her suffer.

The girl in white and I are still holding hands. Neither of us wanted to see or hear that ugly exchange of words.

I brace myself when my mom gets up after a while and goes to Andre's room. I fear more confrontation is on its way. But when she opens the door, instead of clothes and personal belongings being shoved into bags, my brother is just sitting there on his bed, in the same position my mom was in earlier, with his head buried in his hands.

She sits down beside him and then – with her pride left behind in the kitchen – admits that she overreacted by saying, 'I had a terrible day, Andre. I got angry at the office and now I've been forced to take some time off. It was my fault and I took it out on you. I am so sorry.'

'I'm sorry too, but you are not alone. I am also angry.' Andre clenches his teeth then adds, 'I did not want to tell you before, but I got suspended from school two days ago. Some stupid girl thought she could spread rumours about Tom, so I smeared her locker's inside with yogurt.'

My mom begins to laugh, something I haven't seen her do for quite some time. 'Yogurt?' she says incredulously. 'You couldn't have thought about something else? Like chicken shit or molasses, for example?'

When my brother doesn't say anything in return, my mom puts a hand on his cheek and asks, 'What flavour was it?'

'Banana,' he answers.

Now it's my turn to laugh. Because if there is anything in the world that Andre Johnson hates with a passion it's the smell of banana yogurt. I find myself sincerely hoping that the girl who talked crap about me hates it as well.

'Well, apart from your prank idea being awful,' says my mom, 'I am not mad at you for getting suspended.'

'You're not?' my brother asks suspiciously.

'No, Andre, I'm not mad. It's not like I am setting the best example at the moment. And, besides, that girl certainly deserved a locker full of stinking banana yogurt.' She smiles motherly at him. 'But the next time someone agitates you, go to a teacher or speak to me, okay?'

Her voice is reassuring to Andre, I can sense it.

'Well, at least now that we're both sort of "grounded" in a way, we can spend the remainder of the week at home together, doing fun stuff,' he tells her. Then they embrace each other lovingly.

CHAPTER 12

'I'm not going to lie to you, Tom, this part is quite painful,' the girl in white warns me with a stern look in her eyes.

'What is it?' I ask. There is a growing knot in my stomach.

'I want to demonstrate the next stage of grief, bargaining. But before I can show you that, you first need to see and understand the event that led up to it.'

We are now in my bedroom, where my lifeless body is on the bed, the skin a pale blueish. It's rather haunting, like something from a thriller movie. In addition, it feels paranormal, this out-of-body experience. Its reminds me of how dead I actually am. Then something clicks in my mind. Andre hasn't found me yet in this timeline of the vision. According to the digital clock on the bedside table it is about forty minutes after I've taken my last breath.

I begin to wonder how long it took him to find me in the end, but I get the answer soon enough.

A minute later the door is eased open and my brother casually strolls into my room. He has a textbook tucked under his arm and a pencil clenched between his teeth.

'Hey, bro,' he says, still biting down on the pencil. 'Do you have time to help me with this math—'

Then he freezes when he looks at me and registers what he is seeing. The textbook and the pencil drops to the carpet as he rushes towards me, gasping for air.

'Tom!' he yells, while violently shaking my shoulders. 'Wake up! Tom!'

This carries on for a good thirty seconds and then he comes to grips with what has happened. He puts his ear in front of my mouth to hear if I'm breathing. After a short while he shakes his head and presses his thumb against the inner part of my left wrist to feel for a pulse. Finally, once my poor brother has established that there is no life left in my pale body, he pulls his mobile phone from the back pocket of his jeans and starts dialling.

He is quivering so much that the phone slips from his hands twice. When he eventually gets through, he says, 'Mom, you have to come home. Something's wrong with Tom! I think… I think he is dead. Oh, God, please help.' Those are the only four panicked phrases he manages to get out before bursting into a waterfall of tears.

Whilst crying, he's trying everything to revive me. He first performs the only CPR technique he knows by giving me chest compressions at one-second intervals. When that doesn't work he rolls my body over to the side, trying to get the vomit dislodged from my mouth and throat. But I know that these last efforts are futile; I've been as dead as a dodo for more than half an hour on that bed.

The ambulance arrives exactly seven minutes later. The paramedics load my still body onto a fold-up stretcher and then into the back of the van. Andre gets a ride in front.

This is all so completely surreal to watch unfold.

***

At the hospital, my mom arrives to find Andre on a bench in the tiled lobby. He is no longer crying. He just sits there with his hands folded in his lap, grinding his teeth.

'Andre, my baby,' she cries out, throwing her arms around his neck. 'What happened?'

'Tom's room was so quiet, Mom,' he whispers hoarsely. 'There was no sound from the computer or him talking. Why did I not check on him? It is my fault this happened.'

I know that is very difficult for him to say.

'Do not blame yourself,' my mom replies with glistening tears streaming down her face. 'I've spoken to one of the paramedics; he assured me you did everything you could.'

'Clearly it wasn't enough,' my brother says sullenly.

My mom is at a loss for words. I know it when I see it. She is trying to think about what to say but there's nothing. Nothing she says or does will make Andre feel any better.

'It should have been me,' he tells her, looking at his own reflection in the hospital's tall windows.

'Don't ever say that, Andre. It should not have been you, it should not have been him, it shouldn't have happened to anyone. But the world is unfair sometimes.' While she is speaking, it sounds as if she can feel her other son also slipping away through her fingers.

'I just feel so guilty, Mom. Why did I not see that he was so sad and depressed?' He starts crying again.

'I know, sweetheart,' she says, gripping him in her arms like a new-born baby. 'Because I feel the same way.'

They sit like that for a long time, sobbing, until they finally find the strength to stand up and walk out of there. I bet the pain is weighing down on them like ten thousand tons of bricks, trying to suffocate them and then crush them.

CHAPTER 13

Seeing my brother in so much misery, after he found me like that, cuts deeper than any sharp blade ever could.

'If I choose to live, does that still happen to Andre?' I ask the girl in white. I'm feeling tired and deflated.

She makes a sad face. 'Unfortunately, yes. Your brother will always be the one to find you. That won't change.'

I sigh, filled with the knowledge that I can never take back the pain I've caused to my mom and my brother. The only silver lining is that their heartache will fade, just like the girl in white said, and then they'll move on with their lives.

'Okay, I want to see them cheerful,' I tell her.

'You will,' she replies. 'But like I said, I want to show you both sides. So, let's take a look at the bad side now.'

'Wait, that was not it?' I groan, not believing my ears.

'Nope, sorry, Tom. As cruel and painful that was for you to watch, we still have to deal with the two final stages of depression and acceptance. Those are the worst.'

The vision morphs once again, this time to Andre's room. He is now asleep in his bed, although the sun is still shining through the slightly ajar curtains. I consult the time on his cell phone to see that it's not even 3 p.m. yet.

Is he alright? I wonder, suddenly feeling the need to wake him up and tell him to do something productive.

'Are you worried about him?' the girl in white asks, as if it wouldn't be the most obvious feeling in the world for me.

I nod my head, then shake it before saying, 'He can't stay in bed all day. It does not help your mood.' I want to shake him and warn him not to fall into the same habits as mine.

4 p.m. then 5 p.m. and 6 p.m. rolls around and at last he gets up. He stumbles his way downstairs and goes into the kitchen to fix himself a large bowl of cereal, probably his first meal of the day. He sits and watches television until 4 a.m. and then goes to bed again. Life on repeat. Sleep, eat, television. The routine

is so eerily similar to mine, only he's chosen movies and series over video games.

***

Eventually the day arrives when his suspension comes to an end and he goes back to school. Within the first ten minutes of the very first class, he gets called by one of the seniors to visit the guidance counsellor's office.

'How have you been lately, Andre?' the counsellor asks, obviously trying to understand his mental well-being and thereby assess his ability to function normally.

'Fine,' my brother says, refusing to make eye contact.

'Do not feel pressured to do anything you are not ready for yet,' the counsellor suggests. 'If you are, for instance, unable to finish your school work in time, let me know and I will instruct your teachers to extend your deadlines'.

'Fine,' Andre repeats, impatiently. 'Can I go now, sir?'

'Sure,' the guidance counsellor replies with a forced smile. 'Please keep in touch, Andre. Don't be a stranger now.'

***

Over time my brother becomes skinnier and his grades are dropping a bit. Surprisingly not as much as I thought they would, but his 4.0 is now down to a 3.0. My mom tried to talk to him about it on numerous occasions, to no avail. He is gradually becoming a brick wall and nobody is getting through to him anymore.

The girl in white looks at me tenderly, then waves her arm and the vision alters into the school's location once again, the music room to be exact.

My brother's female music teacher sits down next to him behind the piano and says, 'I hear from your mother that you want to quit your piano lessons. You know, you are really talented and it would be a great shame if –'

'I know I know,' he interrupts her. 'Wasted potential and lost opportunities and all that crock of shit.'

She takes a deep breath before continuing. 'Yes, so you know the speech… Look, Andre, I know that you are going through a rough time, but your brother would've wanted you to continue with your passion. You have an excellent chance of getting into Julliard, something you've desired for as long as I've known you. I'm not going to let you give up this easily. So, you are going to come here three times a week after school, like you have always done. I promise you, you will thank me for the good advice one day.'

'You are doing this for you, not for me,' he says angrily.

'Well, you might believe that right now, but in a year's time, when you get accepted to your dream college it will all be worth it. Only then will you see who it benefits.'

Andre quickly rises to his feet and then storms out of the music class without saying anything else or looking back. It takes him less than ten minutes to ride home on his bicycle. He hurries to his bedroom where he starts playing mindless level-up games on his cell phone.

Moments later my mom walks into the room.

'I have someone here who wants to see you,' she says, making way for none other than Jake to enter.

My heart swells with pride. I'm so happy to know that my best friend is looking out for my brother.

'Hey man,' Jake says with a friendly face. Behind him, my mother quietly slips out through the door.

'Hi,' Andre responds from where he's sitting on the bed. He briefly looks up from his phone's screen.

Jake leans over to study the phone. 'You know I love that game. It's quite addictive. Emma and I play it all the time.'

'You're not here to talk about games, are you?' Andre says with an ominous sneer.

'No,' Jake admits, seating himself on the edge of the bed. 'I'm here because I'm worried about you. I mean, it's not a good thing to shut society out the way you do.'

Andre puts the phone down on the bedside table and then meets Jake's gaze. 'You know what, Jake? I simply can't stand the sympathy stares that people give me any longer. It's been almost a year and they still look at me, thinking, *Shame, that's the poor dude who lost his bro.*'

'I feel you, man,' Jake replies. 'I get the same looks, but can I tell you a secret? They hurt me more when I viewed myself as they guy who lost his best friend. Nowadays I just try to remember that I can help others because of the lessons I've learned from my experience. The people out there don't understand that they are not helping with their condescending looks, but you have to remember something, Andre: That is not their intention. Not at all.'

'You're most likely right,' Andre responds, tears welling up in his eyes. 'But it's still so damn hard, man.'

'I know, and the only thing you can do is to hold onto the people you care about and who care about you in return.' Jake places a hand on Andre's leg and holds it there.

I watch as a thin smile slowly grows on my brother's lips, hoping that he is finally going to be okay.

CHAPTER 14

'We are almost through the five stages of guilt,' says the girl in white. 'How are you doing, Tom?'

'Actually, I thought I would be feeling a lot worse than I am at the moment. I'm a little light-headed and drained of energy, but otherwise I'm alright. And I think my family and friends are also going to be okay.'

'Yes, they will be okay, but it doesn't mean that you won't be missed, or that your lack of presence won't be noticed. You are also going to miss out on so much of their lives.'

'Do you want me to feel sad or something?' I ask in a grim voice. 'Is that what this is? A guilt trip?'

'I don't know what it is,' she replies, 'but I certainly do not want you to feel guilty or sad. Having said that, I also don't think it's good that you're so pleased with your choice to leave everyone behind on earth while you go into the afterlife. I'm not sure you understand what you are giving up, or the potential your life has for that matter.'

I study her body language for a second before speaking again. 'I am not you. You don't know for sure that my life will get better if I go back to live it. And just because you regret *your* decision doesn't mean I regret mine.'

She looks the other way and I see her upset and dejected for the first time.

I step around her to make eye contact and then I say, in my sincerest voice, 'I'm sorry. I am just seriously confused right now and I'm not sure what you want me to do.'

She finally looks at me with those emerald green eyes. 'The truth is, you are right. I do regret my decision, but for one reason only. I might tell you at a later stage, we'll see. For now, I simply want you to comprehend the difference between you being there for your friends and family, and you *not* being there for them.'

I smile at her for repeating herself so often.

I sometimes forget that she is human too – *was* human too. But still, her beauty, wisdom and kindness surpasses everything I would expect from any other person, save for Emma perhaps. I hug the girl in white to show her that we are good and that there is no bad blood between us.

'Before we continue I want to tell you a story,' she informs me, pulling herself together.

'Go ahead,' I reply. I'm always a sucker for stories.

The girl in white speaks with animated arms. 'Back in the days when an ice-cream sundae cost much less than today, a seven-year-old boy walked into a waffle house and sat down at one of the tables. A waitress approached him and asked what he would like to order. Studying the ice-cream pictures on the wall, he asked, "How much is an ice-cream sundae?" "Fifty cents," the waitress replied. The boy retrieved a handful of coins from his pocket and started counting. After a while, he looked up and asked, "How much is a bowl of plain ice-cream?" The waitress told him, "Thirty-five cents," in a callous voice. The boy counted the coins again and then said, "I'll have the plain ice-cream, thank you, Miss."

'The waitress brought the ice-cream and the bill a few minutes later, and she left the boy to enjoy his treat in peace. He ate his ice-cream, savouring every moment, and then stood up. He paid at the cashier counter and left the waffle house. When the waitress cleared the table afterwards, she stood there with a big lump in her throat. Beside the empty ice-cream bowl was a neatly stacked heap of coins, totalling fifteen cents – her tip…'

'That's a beautiful story,' I hear myself mutter.

The girl in white wrinkles her nose. 'I told you the story because *you* were that boy once, Tom Johnson.'

I have no response to that. I'm ill-equipped to handle such compliments, therefore I only bob my head up and down.

'Are you ready for the next scene of life for others without you in the world?' she asks with raised eyebrows.

'Yeah, I am ready,' I reply, now getting used to the visions.

The room begins to spin again and then we are back in my mom's house, in the living room. However, there are a few minor changes to what I've seen at my family's first Christmas without me. A new coffee table, a bigger vase of flowers on the mantelpiece, thicker curtains, and a new row of framed photographs against the wall, with spaces of exactly two feet between each of them.

Andre and my mom are sitting on one of the couches with cups of tea in their hands, and the television is playing in the background. The first thing I notice is the absolute joy on their faces. They are talking and laughing about fond memories. Memories of me, I soon find out.

'Do you remember the time Tom tried to balance on the chair in that restaurant and fell backwards?' my mother recalls, her face beaming. 'It was like he was falling in slow motion and you could see his eyes widen and his mouth gape when he realised he messed up.'

They laugh even harder at the thought of my stunned facial expression on that day. Their laughter makes me feel so blissful, knowing they can look back and think about funny moments from our past.

Just as Andre is about to share another memory with my mom, the room dissipates, first turning into a cloud of smoke and then transforming into a bare bedroom – my bedroom. All the furniture has been removed and on the floor stands an array of paint buckets.

They are finally redecorating the place, I think to myself. *That is a step in the right direction.*

The once blue walls are now white, except for the one to the left of the door, which contains decorative wallpaper, also white, with pastel blue diagonal lines.

Blue has always been my favourite colour.

***

The scene jumps to another three months later.

My brother and my mom are walking into the house, but this time they have a cute companion with them.

'Look, Babadook, this is your new home,' Andre says, cuddling a silver-grey kitten so tiny it looks like a stuffed toy. Its bright eyes are darting around the living room to figure out where these friendly giants are relocating it to.

My brother sets the little guy down, and he cautiously tiptoes around on the wooden floor. My mom is carrying his bed and his toys in her arms. She asks Andre to fetch the tins of cat food from the car in the driveway.

After exploring the lounge for a while, Babadook walks up the stairs and then straight to my old room. He cautiously enters through the open door, then jumps onto the single bed that has now replaced my queen-size double bed.

My mom follows the adorable kitten and asks, 'Do you like this room, Babadook?'

The kitten cocks its head to the side.

'It is...' my mom begins, then she pauses to think for a moment and says, 'It used to be my other son's bedroom,' as if the cat can understand her. 'I miss him, every day.'

She sits down next to Babadook and takes a deep breath. 'I wish you could have met him,' she says sadly. She is close to tears but not crying yet.

Babadook shuffles towards her and then rolls into her lap, seemingly sympathising with her, almost as if he *could* actually understand what she was telling him.

Downstairs, my brother opens a tin of cat food and carefully empties the contents into Babadook's stainless steel bowl before saying, 'At least now we're three in the house again. Three's company…'

CHAPTER 15

Andre is running down the sunlit street as fast as his legs can possibly carry him.

With each step of his rubber soles slapping down onto the tarmac, it looks like he is going to lift from the ground and magically start flying to his final destination. His intense, rhythmic breaths are ever increasing in rapidness and drops of perspiration is rolling down the nape of his neck.

Six minutes later he finally slows down as he reaches the end of his journey, the serene front porch of our house. He swings the front door open, panting. After standing with his hands on his knees in the doorway for a while, he looks up. His eyes instantly lock on his target – my mom, sitting at the dinner table with an ear-to-ear grin.

'It has arrived?' he asks impatiently, still out of breath.

'It's right here,' she tells him, holding up a crisp envelope, addressed to my brother.

He rushes to the table and snatches the manila envelope from her hands in pure excitement. He takes a seat next to her and stares at the enclosed letter, studying the typed letters that spell out his name and address.

'Whenever you are ready, son,' my mom says, touching his elbow with her beautiful hand.

Andre tears open the envelope, rips out the letter and unfolds it. His eyes are fiercely scanning the document clenched in his hands. Then he whispers, 'I got in.'

'What did you say?' my mom asks, growing in elation.

'I got in,' he repeats, much louder and now with an air of confidence in his voice.

'You got in!' my mom shouts. 'I knew you would get in!'

She cannot hide her pride as she hurries to the fridge in the kitchen and yanks out a vanilla cake. She obviously bought it, since my mom can't bake to save her life.

On top of the spongy cake the words 'Julliard Art School' are written in turquoise frosting and below it, in black-and-gold frosting, 'Congratulations, Tom!'

I feel a warming glow in my cheeks to see my mother so utterly gratified and ecstatic. Andre is dancing behind her, spinning about and waving his now quite crumpled letter around in the air above his head.

'I have to text my music teacher,' he says, producing his phone from his pocket. 'I owe her so much.'

Once he has sent the longest thank you text message I've ever seen, he turns to our mother, saying, 'I would not have been able to do this without you either, Mom. Thank you for always being in my corner and for helping me with the application forms and everything.'

She smiles at him, clearly touched by his sweet words, and then they collide together in a warm embrace.

***

The day of my brother's enrolment in college arrives.

Unfamiliar faces from all over the country are rocking up at the Julliard Arts Conservatory in New York City.

The scene at Andre's new fraternity house is jovial. There are students hugging their parents and waving goodbye as the cars disappear into the distance. Young adults are carrying twice their weight in boxes, lugging them up the stairs while trying to swerve past other students, clumsily avoiding a collision on their first day.

Andre takes the medium-sized suitcase (which all his clothes managed to fit into) out of the rental car's trunk, and my mom carries his box of shoes as they make their way across the patch of lawn in front of his new home.

I can't believe my brother is finally going to attend college. A feeling of excitement mixed with fear for him is washing over me. This is a wonderful day for the Johnsons and I'm so glad for Andre. I know he'll make a success out of it and will one day carve a name for himself in the competitive music world. All the hard work of going to auditions and filling out applications is now eventually paying off.

Once he and my mom have carried everything up to the dorm room, they simultaneously sit down on the single bed, still with the plastic mattress protector covering it.

'How are you feeling, son?' my mother asks.

I know she's trying to hide her unavoidable melancholy, since her son is no longer going to live under the same roof as her. She will now be spending her time in an empty nest, not able to see him every day anymore.

'I'm not sure what to make of it all, Mom,' Andre answers. A nervous chortle escapes his mouth. 'I felt like I was ready for this for quite some time, but now that the day has come and we are here I feel a bit apprehensive.'

My mom squints. 'About what? You know everyone will love you and you will make new friends in no time.'

'I'm worried about leaving you,' Andre admits, rubbing his chin. 'Are you going to be okay on your own?'

I'm deeply touched by my brother's concern for her and not himself. He has grown into a great guy.

'Don't you worry about me, young man,' says my mom. 'Now that I have the TV to myself, I can watch all my soap operas without having to share them with that MTV crap you're always watching.'

Andre first chuckles, then his face turns serious. 'Just focus on yourself and all the amazing things you are still going to achieve in life, Mom. I am so incredibly proud of you. You are one of the strongest people I know and I hope I can apply some of your knowledge and ability here, so that when I graduate I will also be a stronger person.'

It's a weird situation. The parent is supposed to teach the child, but I think for Andre it is the other way around for some or other reason.

They say their goodbyes, albeit only temporary, and then my mother is on her way back to the airport, leaving behind a nervous but motivated Andre. At least those are the emotions I pick up from his brotherly vibes.

Chapter 16

'You see? They are better off without me,' I tell the girl in white. 'Look at how well they are doing.'

'Tom, you don't have the bigger picture yet,' she says in a droning monotone voice.

'Of course I have. I've just witnessed it in that vision about Andre going to college. They got over my death, both my brother and my mom. They don't have that sorrow and heartache anymore, and they won't have to live with such burdens forever, unlike me if I decide to go back.'

The girl in white stares at me with a rather emotionless expression, then says, 'I'm confused. What do you mean?'

'What I'm trying to tell you is that the pain will never go away for *me*. I'll always have that crushing feeling inside, my whole entire life.'

She smiles at me, finally showing some emotion. 'First of all,' she says, 'you cannot use "whole" and "entire" in the same sentence. Second of all, pain will always be a part of your life, Tom. You can't avoid it, but when it is in balance with the joyful moments, that pain becomes a blur.'

'Okay,' I say tentatively. 'But what if it doesn't? What if all there is to my future is agony? Or misery? Or whatever?'

She rubs her temples with her thumbs before speaking in a voice barely above a whisper. 'Let us take a look at the future. And I mean much further into the future. From four years since your death to forty years on.'

'You want to show me my entire future? Spoil my whole life so that I don't have to experience it? Do you think that will convince me not to stay here?' I smirk at her.

'No, silly,' she smirks back. 'I'm only going to show you *one* possible future. One path, that may or may not happen. Perhaps certain elements of that path will come true while other parts will not, or maybe none of what I show will be in your future. But the possibility is there.'

'So, essentially, it's guesswork?'

'Not entirely,' replies the girl in white. 'Everyone's future is carved out before they are even born. This carving is made up of many different branches, like a massive tree. While you live, every branch will either fall away or come true based on the choices you make at each crossroad.'

Now I almost understand. This girl really wants to help me but she is struggling to get her point across. The tree branch example makes a lot of sense. She can't show me everything, but she can show me bits and pieces. And she has done so with tremendous kindness thus far.

I just wish I can somehow repay her kindness, but I don't even know her name… or what she is…

CHAPTER 17

As time goes by, my people heal. Slowly but surely.

Jake and Emma are thriving in their relationship, Andre is doing well in college and my mom is back at the office.

My mom has now also found purpose in a life that was once repetitive, as she's discovered a new way to cope with her grief. She has launched a charity organisation called Lucy Loves Life. The organisation deals with mental health issues for all ages, with a toll-free helpline to call.

People can phone in and get help when they feel anxious and alone or in distress. My mom has employed enough social workers, so there is always someone on the other end of the line to listen and assist callers in any way they can. Because of the overwhelming success of Lucy Loves Life, volunteers are now also knocking on my mother's door, ready to accept calls from people reaching out for help at any hour of the day.

The charity organisation soon raises enough money to open an overnight hotel, a venture brought on by another volunteer; a generous hotel owner who closed off several floors of his establishment. The LLL hotel section provides a shelter for people who don't want to be alone for the night. They can now go to a safe haven to breathe and relax. The hotel owner – currently my mom's partner in her business – told her his own story of how his younger sister had committed suicide six years earlier.

Courtesy of the girl in white's visions, I find out how many people are actually suffering from suicidal depression. There are hundreds and thousands of them. A daughter here, a brother there, a work colleague or a close friend. There is always someone.

I guess I was not as alone in my miserable life after all.

***

One afternoon my mom is having a sit-down with the hotel owner, chatting over coffee in a pretty little café not far from the hotel itself.

The café features grey-painted cedar wood tables with matching chairs, sitting on white tiled floors. The walls are also white with Cerise pink decorations. When coffee is served, the milk comes in cute miniature milk bottles and the coffee in retro navy-blue ceramic mugs.

'Lucy, may I ask you how you came up with the idea of the overnight facility?' the hotel owner asks, speaking very politely to my mother.

She cradles the coffee mug in her hands. 'Originally I only aspired to raise awareness about suicidal tendencies, but over the years I figured out that a lot of that is on account of people being alone, especially at night time.'

'That sounds familiar,' he says. 'People didn't understand why my sister, uhm, why she did what she did. But the more I think about it, the more I realise how alone she was in the world. I should have reached out but I didn't.'

'I know the feeling,' my mom replies, nodding. 'Someone at the office where I work also didn't understand, and a lot of Andre's school teachers were less than supportive. To be honest, I was like that as well in the beginning – oblivious, I mean – but now that I've experienced losing my son to the claws of suicide, I've become more open-minded and empathetic to the whole subject.'

The hotel owner takes a careful sip of his over-priced coffee before saying, 'You're a fantastic woman, Lucy. I'm blessed to have you as a business partner.'

Two tables behind them an elderly woman whispers in her husband's ear, 'Isn't that the hotel magnate originally from San Francisco? I hear he's a millionaire now.'

The conversation between my mom and the 'millionaire' continues for another hour and then he has to leave to attend to his hotel's financial matters. Before he walks out of the café, he turns nervously and stutters, 'I... I was wondering if... if maybe you would want to go out for dinner with me at some point this week?'

'Yes, I would love that,' my mom replies.

Visibly thrilled by her answer he says, 'Great, how about Thursday? I'll pick you up at seven.'

She blushes. 'Sure, Thursday sounds great.'

'I'll see you then,' he says, and walks through the door and into the chilly morning air.

CHAPTER 18

'I think it's time to go even further into the future,' the girl in white says, cutting the café scene short.

'It may not be my future though,' I tell her.

'No, but that does not mean you don't want to see it.'

'I am more worried that if I choose to live I won't be happy with the final outcome. Or if it *is* my future we're talking about, that I will already know the outcome and therefore live a seriously boring life.'

She thinks for a while and then replies, 'It could be a possibility, but it will definitely not be the exact outcome I'm showing you. There are thousands of possible futures. The one I'm about to lay out will start as a story about you and then become a vision. If you choose not to die, this story can turn into reality and your actual experience will have lots of personal connections and first moments. That's why a decision against dying will be better than merely hearing or seeing the story. However, the actual purpose of the story is to show you that pain goes away, then comes back and then disappears again.'

'Okay, let's hear it then,' I demand, but in a playful tone.

'Well, in this possible future you find a partner. Her name is Alex, and you will have three beautiful children with her, two girls and a boy. The boy is the youngest and rather sweet, like his dad. The other member of your family is a dog, a German Shepherd named Yuki.'

'That is a cool name,' I interrupt, laughing, 'It rolls nicely off the tongue: "Yuki." But I can't see myself thinking of a name like that. Alex must have chosen it.'

'Yeah, spot on,' the girl in white confirms. 'Anyway, the rest of the story will now appear as a vision.'

'Wait.' I hold up a hand, palm facing forward. 'I need a minute to prepare myself.'

'Take all the time you need, Tom.'

Her compassion is quite refreshing, as always. I don't feel pressured to act different around her. She accepts me for who I am and that is totally unlike my bad experience of seventeen years in the real world.

'Thank you,' I say. 'I appreciate it.'

While sitting down, I can feel how tense the muscles in my lower back are. With me being dead I can't understand how that is even possible but the stiffness is there, just the same, almost overwhelming. It's been an exhausting day and I know at the very end I must still make a huge decision. That's a bit of a dilemma, because I'm not even close to knowing what to choose yet.

The silence while I'm sitting and thinking is peaceful. In other situations, such a long silence would feel awkward and uncomfortable, but not with the girl in white.

'Alright, I'm ready,' I inform her after meditating for ten minutes. I jump to my feet, feeling energised again.

'Are you sure?' she asks. 'There is no rush.'

'I am ready, thank you. And I'm not scared, because you are going to be right by my side the whole way.'

She looks at me with a smile playing across her lips. 'I'm glad I make you feel calm and secure, Tom.'

Chapter 19

I smell the ocean, salty and humid. A strong gust of wind strikes my face and I can see a seagull flying overhead. Its squawks gradually become softer and softer until it's only a small dot in sky. The puffy white clouds against the bright blue atmosphere reminds me of a child's drawing. My bare feet sink into the soft sand and it envelopes them as if it were the world's most comfortable shoes.

I tear my eyes away from the picturesque scene and look down to find a line of paw prints running along the shore. Playing around in the shallow water, with a wooden stick in its mouth, is a healthy German Shepherd. Every once in a while it looks back at its owners, presumably to make sure they are still here. And that is when my gaze shifts to my own older image, walking down the beach with a lady, holding hands and laughing.

A while later, my future self starts running, chased by Alex until she catches me and pushes me to the ground. I grunt as I fall, face down, and then laugh as we roll around, with Yuki jumping over us, barking and wagging his tail.

After getting back onto our feet, we dust the sand from our beachwear and then walk to an ice-cream kiosk on the pier. I buy us cold drinks to quench our thirst and I ask the cashier for a bowl of water for Yuki.

'That is so sweet,' the girl in white says, giving me a light-hearted punch on my upper arm.

'You think?' I reply, attempting to deny the fact that I love this memory I've never actually had.

'Do you want to see the day you bought Yuki?' she asks.

'Sure. That'll be great.'

Moments later we are in a noisy pet shop, staring at a litter of puppies. All of them are sort of dancing, happy and excited, but one in particular stands out. The way it wiggles its bottom and spins around – almost as if it is proud to be the bad dancer in the group – is adorable. Its personality elevates above the other puppies and Alex and I instantly know that it's going to be our dog.

Alex picks it up and she giggles as it squirms around in her hands, looking like a fluffy propeller on a speed boat. She passes him to me as I sit down next to them.

I make eye contact with the puppy and it feels like we've known each other for years. Dog. A man's best friend.

'Yuki,' Alex's voice whispers. 'He looks like a Yuki.'

'That's just the perfect name for him,' I respond, whilst hugging both Alex and our new dog; the first addition to our family.

***

Time moves on and birthdays, holidays and late nights go by. The more days that pass, the more traditions Alex and I form. Like taking Yuki for a walk in the botanical garden every Monday morning, or ordering lamb curry (from the take-out place around the corner from our house) every thanksgiving, because neither me nor Alex can cook even basic food. We would always dry out the turkey, burn the potatoes and spoil the sauce by adding too much flour.

***

The day finally arrives where we hold hands and say our vows in front of all our family and friends. The day a legal document binds us together and we are a married couple. All night everyone dances, which gets increasingly worse the more alcohol is ingested. The bar is stocked with beer, wine, champagne and liquor such as whisky and rum.

My navy suit, matched with brown shoes and a brown belt, makes me look sophisticated. Jake, my best man of course, is wearing a pristine black tuxedo Emma picked out for him. My mom and Andre is dancing in the centre of the floor, not caring what people think about them. They are jiving and boogying like nobody's business. Her long red dress flutters with every turn and I can see that the dancing is making her feel young again.

It turns out to be my absolute dream wedding.

***

A year passes and I walk into our home one day.

I watch myself set down bags of groceries on the kitchen counter, so much of them that I drop the dog food on the floor. Yuki is jumping up and down in excitement.

It's so completely bizarre to see myself living the life of an adult. I'm madly in love, cheerful, and ageing well.

My future self kneels down and pets Yuki with a smile. 'Now you are going to see something for the first time and I need you to stay calm. You cannot be the usual over-dramatic Yuki, understand?'

His ears twitch in confusion, and that's when Alex walks in with our new-born baby girl. She is so tiny and delicate, with her eyes still closed, ignoring life around her. Why? Because my beautiful daughter has no responsibilities or concerns in the world. Not yet, anyway.

Chapter 20

Alex and the older version of myself cross the street on a mild but breezy autumn afternoon. Orange-brown leaves are swirling around on the sidewalk like low-flying birds.

We have just arrived at the restaurant where Jake and Emma are already waiting outside. Emma is hopping up and down to keep herself warm in her purple dress, not a suitable outfit for such a windy day. Jake is in a cream button-down shirt and formal trousers, proving that the restaurant we're dining at is a fancy one. He always wears casual clothes like jeans and t-shirts, even to an interview earlier in the year. But it didn't matter because he still got the job, using his vast social and interpersonal skills.

'Hi, guys,' he now says, shaking my hand while at the same time hugging Alex hello.

'Hey, you look nice for a change,' my future self tells him.

Emma snickers under her breath and Alex puts a gloved hand over her mouth.

'Good of you to eventually show up,' says Jake, ignoring the silly remark. 'I'm quite surprised that my poor Emma hasn't died of hyperthermia yet,' he jests.

'Certain ladies are always fashionably late,' I joke back, pointing a thumb at Alex.

She chuckles. 'Yeah, says the handsome gentleman who couldn't pick one of five different ties.'

We all laugh at how none of our personalities have really changed that much over all the years.

We go inside, sit down at a booth in the back and order drinks. Alex and Jake decide on beer, while Emma and I opt for white wine. For starters the four of us share a seafood platter with prawns, mussels, crab sticks and hake medallions, all served with a creamy garlic and lemon sauce. For mains we all order the house speciality: beef fillet with sautéed mushrooms. We end up spending hours eating, drinking and talking. There are just so many stories to share.

Alex tells them about how we met each other, dancing at a rave party in college, and how I spilled my drink over her best friend's blouse. Alex's friend then tossed her drink over me and Alex helped me clean up afterwards.

We speak about how Jake and Emma went abroad for a month, travelling to Greece, Spain, Portugal and then the United Kingdom. They show us photographs and voice their stories of the eccentric people they've met along the way. They befriended a Spanish couple and can now stay with them in their villa when they visit and vice versa.

Jake suggests that we should all go on a trip together, the four of us and Rhys.

'Maybe Norway or Iceland,' Emma proposes in a high-pitched voice, evidently excited about the prospect.

We also establish a new monthly event called music night. The location will alternate between our homes and the idea is for everyone to choose five of their favourite songs in a certain genre. We'll listen to all twenty songs and then vote for the best three of the night. By the end of the year, the winning songs of each month will be compiled into a playlist and aired on Jake's podcast.

I am grateful for friends and loved ones who are keeping me busy and happy. Nevertheless, this is one day out of many that could potentially be awful. I decide to disclose my opinion to the girl in white.

'Showing me one good day does not help,' I whine.

'No it doesn't,' she admits. 'That is why the next part is going to be tough on your emotions. It is time to show you one of the worst days of your life.'

I clench my fists before saying, 'I can do this.'

'I know you can,' she comforts me.

CHAPTER 21

The vision shifts to a hospital ward where my mom is in bed, dying. Andre and the hotel owner are sitting in plastic chairs on either side of the bed. Dozens of cords, leading to monitoring equipment, are attached to her chest and arms. An intravenous drip is providing pain medication and there are oxygen tubes attached to her nose.

With each rasping breath she takes there is a longer gap between inhaling and exhaling. I can see on the monitors that her heart rate is slowing rapidly.

Three minutes later, she takes one last struggling breath and then it is all over.

My brother puts his head down on the bed beside her and his shoulders begin to shake as he first weeps then bawls. The hotel owner is soon crying with him.

My eyes are also filling up with tears. Seeing my mom pass away is harder than I anticipated. I try to hug Andre but he cannot not feel my embrace.

'I'm right here, little brother,' I say to him. 'I am with you.'

I stare at my mother's fragile body in dismay. I could not be there for her when she passed away. And even though the thought is insanely painful, I now know that I want to be there in person when it happens. For two reasons: first so that she knows I'm sharing her final moments with her, and second so that I can support Andre when she goes.

I collapse to the ground, disheartened, because I couldn't be there with my brother and my mom. Also, because I know that they felt this same pain when I died. If they experienced even an ounce of the agony I'm suffering right now, I understand everything. Why they got so angry, why Andre became depressed, why my mom was so sad on Christmas day. I understand everything now.

'I'm sorry about this,' the girl in white says to me. Her face is pallid and her lips are parched.

'I get why you're showing me this,' I tell her, standing up and wiping away my tears.

She shrugs her shoulders. 'Not everything in life is joyful, Tom, and you are now here in one of the worst moments. Yet, you survived it. I saw how you wanted to hold Andre, how you wanted to be there for him.'

'Of course I wanted to. Did you see how shattered he was? I wanted to support him, because it might have been the worst moment in my life but it was also his.'

'Other stages of life will not be perfect either,' the girl in white states. 'But you have proven to yourself that you can get through the difficult times. You will always get over these stumbling blocks, even if they have nothing to do with someone's death.'

'Like what?' I ask in anticipation.

'Let me take you there,' she tells me.

The vision fades to black and opens in my future self's kitchen, yours truly standing opposite Alex.

We are in a heated argument because, according to this version of me, Alex is spending too much time at work.

'I need to focus on my career, you know that!' Alex yells.

'It would be nice if you could at least come home before it gets dark, considering you leave before dawn every morning!' my future self yells back in frustration.

She slams a palm against the fridge. 'Damn it, Tommy! We agreed you would take care of the kids while I'm working my ass off. I'm doing this for *us*, you know?'

I see myself grimace in the vision. 'Well, Alexandra, if "doing this for us" is always going to entail spending more than twelve hours at work every day, then I'd rather be piss poor thank you!'

'I am not dealing with this right now,' she says with even more anger in her usually loving voice. 'It's not my fault that you didn't want to discuss the details of my workload before we decided that you were going to be a stay-at-home dad. This conversation is over!'

'Are you okay?' the girl in white asks me. She must have seen how my mind got carried away with the fight I didn't even pick.

'Wow, that was intense,' I say, shaking my head to get rid of the ugly memory. 'I forgot that a marriage is not always a fairy-tale from a storybook.'

'That is true,' she agrees. 'However, had I not stopped that scene, you would have seen that you guys survive the fight. You also survive many more and end up staying happily married for almost an eternity in this reality.'

CHAPTER 22

'What? Are you going to show me every good moment I missed as well as every bad one?'

She sighs. 'No, these were merely a few examples, Tom. It teaches us something. If you don't experience the pain of loss when someone you love dies, it means that you've never experienced love itself. The same with arguments. Love comes with pain. You cannot have one and not the other, they come as a pair. That is life, take it or leave it.'

A cold look of recognition rolls over her face and I know she is reflecting back on the life she once had.

'You know how I said no one was there to show me what I'm now showing you?' she says, her lower lip trembling. 'When I died...' Her words trail off.

'What happened to you when you reached the space between?' I ask quietly.

'I was alone until I turned around, but then I did not see a stranger. I saw my body. Then I saw *him*.'

She tells me about her sad memory...

'Hi, sweetie,' my father said as he walked into my room. 'I've been calling you for dinner.' Then he saw my dead body on the carpet. The daughter he had raised and loved, now pale with foam around the mouth and eyes rolled back in their sockets. He screamed as he fell down beside me. This loud scream vibrated through my ears. It was an endless sound and you could hear the dense pain in his voice. He held me tight, trying to transfer the life from his body into mine, but he obviously could not do that. All he could do was cry and cry, because he had lost his kind and caring daughter. The only emotion in that room that day was terrible agony. Agony that was so heavy in the air that it pushed me to my knees. All I could do was watch as my dad's face contorted while he wailed and wailed more.

'I wish I could tell him how sorry I am,' the girl in white says, crying. 'I never wanted him to feel that pain.'

Her arm twitches, seemingly involuntarily, and a vision of her room plays out before us.

There are two of her. One is dead on the carpet and the other one is standing behind a clear screen that looks like it used to be a wall. This image of her is banging on the screen while witnessing her dad finding her body.

'I'm sorry, dad!' she screams over and over again.

She did not get the same opportunity I am so fortunate to now have in my hands. She did not get to see her future and she wasn't offered a second chance to live. She was trapped behind a thick see-through screen and she could do nothing about her suicide. No second chances for her...

'I am so sorry that's what happened to you after you died,' I say, feeling horrible.

She wipes her nose with the back of her hand. 'I just wanted to make sure he was okay and that he would be fine without me. I wanted him to know that it was not his fault and that there was nothing he could have done. I just wanted him to know that I loved him so much and that he was the best dad in the world.'

The vision changes once more and we are back in the white empty room where I arrived first.

'Why did you kill yourself?' I ask, unable to stop myself.

'It does not matter,' she says, using her favourite phrase. 'Every suicide is unique, you of all people should know that, Tom. Yes, the result is the same, but the reasons and the feelings behind it are unique. Maybe I observed someone die, maybe I was responsible for someone else's death. Maybe I was bullied, maybe I was abused or maybe I was just genetically predisposed to be sad and lonely. Maybe I was stressed or struggled financially, or maybe there was no reason to feel so low because my life was perfect. It does not matter now.' She bites on her fingernails. '*Suicide isn't an option.* God I hate that saying. as if suicide is like a decision to go left or right.'

The irony of the statement sends a shiver of realisation down my spine. How sickeningly true it is all of a sudden resonates through me. I realise that the world knows shit when it comes to the real struggle and immense pain of someone who goes through the thoughts of ending it all. How truly unaware and uninformed the world is.

'It's a struggle,' the girl in white continues, echoing my thoughts. 'A constant fight not to go that far, not stop battling with the thought. That is what it is, a battle. It's not a road we choose to take. It's a battle of us fighting our demons, and occasionally they win. They knock us down so hard that we cannot fight back anymore. We no longer have the energy to throw another punch.'

'Thank you for saying that,' I say to her 'It's exactly what I've been thinking.'

She puts both her hands on my shoulders and speaks slowly. 'It is time to make your decision, Tom Johnson.'

'Okay, but before I give you my answer can I ask you one thing, please?'

'Anything,' she replies, looking me straight in the eyes.

I hesitate before asking, 'What is your name? I know it doesn't matter to you anymore, but it matters to me. I've grown pretty close to you and you've helped me a lot, so I would like to know what your name is.'

She gives me a bright smile. 'It's Haley.'

'Haley. That's a lovely name.'

'Thank you, but now it's your turn to answer my question. What is your final choice?'

'I have decided to live, Haley,' I tell her. It feels good to call her by her name. 'I need to give my life a chance and I want to experience both the love and pain. I need to be there when my mom passes away, right by her side along with my brother. I want to watch Andre grow into a man, watch Emma and Jake fall in love, watch myself fall in love and get married. But not from an outsider's perspective.'

Haley smiles again. 'I think those are amazing reasons to choose life and I know you are going to do great. You are such a cool, funny and caring guy and I'm genuinely ecstatic with your decision. I wish you the best of luck and, believe me, you are going to make such a difference to so many people in the world.'

Her words are touching my heart. It's something I've never felt before and it's extraordinarily special.

'I honestly have you to thank for it,' I acknowledge. 'You saved me, Haley. Thank you from the bottom of my heart.'

We hug one final time and then she swiftly disappears into thin air.

CHAPTER 23

I open my eyes to see a female face, wearing glasses and a disposable surgical mask. The sharp smell of antiseptics and iodine is creeping up my nostrils.

I'm in a hospital. *Thank you, Haley!*

'He's awake, Doctor,' says the nurse who is staring at me.

'Hello, Tom. I am Doctor Sheffield.' This coming from a friendly male voice to my left. 'How do you feel?'

I slowly turn my head to see a tall man in lime-green scrubs under a white overcoat. 'Where is my mom?' I ask him, slobbering a little.

'She and your brother are in the family waiting room outside. I wanted to wait until you were conscious. Would you like to see them now?'

'Yes, please. If that's alright,' I respond. I'm rather nervous because I don't know what the hell I'm going to say to them. My tummy is aching, from anxiety but also from the feeling of having my stomach pumped.

A minute later, my mom comes rushing into the room like Wonder Woman. She leaps onto me and holds me in a tight grip. 'I'm so sorry, son!' she cries out.

'It's not your fault, Mom. I'm gonna be okay.'

She releases the grip and takes my face in her hands. 'I didn't even know you were feeling like that, my poor boy. I promise I'm going to try harder to be a better mother.'

'There was nothing you could have done,' I tell her, 'but I am better now, I've have had some time to think.'

She frowns. 'You've had some time to think?'

'Yeah, Mom. It's difficult to explain. All you need to know is that my thinking has made me understand a number of truths about human behaviour. I'm going to make a few changes and then I'll be able to do this... this life thing.'

'As long as you are okay now,' she says. 'All I care about is that you get better and feel relaxed.'

Andre has also snuck into the room and is now standing behind her. He's been dead quiet (excuse then pun) so I decide to break the silence.

'I'm so sorry you had to find me like that, bro,' I apologise with sincerity.

Andre gawks at me in confusion. 'How do you know I found you?' he asked, raising his eyebrows.

Realising my mistake, I reply with: 'Just a guess… Or call it brotherly instinct if you will.'

He takes a step forward and hugs me, even tighter than my mom did. It feels good, I'm not going to lie. I am simply so grateful to be close to my family again.

'I want to get help,' I tell my mom. 'Perhaps go to therapy.'

Her face is radiating kindness when she says, 'I think that might be a good idea. Whatever makes you feel the most comfortable and protected.'

'Thanks, Mom. I know I don't always show appreciation for the things you do for me, but that's going to change.'

'Don't worry about that right now,' she replies, squeezing my hand the way only a mother can.

Then a recollection from Haley's visions pops into my head and I say, 'You know what? Maybe we should set up a charity organisation to help people like me.'

Her eyes light up. 'I think that's a great idea! And I love you for coming up with such a generous gesture.'

'It's more your inspiration than my idea,' I tell her, trying to be as cryptic as possible.

***

'Where are we going?' my mom asks as I drag her along to a tall building, five blocks from our house.

Whether it's by a miracle or by fate, I don't know, but the hotel owner steps out the front door just as we get there.

'Hello, I'm Tom,' I greet him.

'Hello, young man,' he returns, fumbling in his jacket pocket until he finds his glasses and puts them on.

'I've heard about your efforts to help people who are feeling depressed and suicidal,' I inform him.

His eyes widen behind the thick glasses. 'Oh, why thank you,' he says. 'I am surprised you have heard about that. I try to keep my involvement quiet so that people don't think I'm doing it for the publicity.'

'Well, I really appreciate it,' I say, then turn to my mother. '*We* really appreciate it. This is my mom, Lucy.'

'Hi there, Lucy' the hotel owner says, taking her hand. 'My name is Phil. What a splendid dress you are wearing.'

'Hello, Phil,' she replies. Her face is flushing. 'Thank you for the compliment. You're a real gentleman.'

CHAPTER 24

'She wants you to know how sorry she is,' I say to the man with the golden-brown hair. He also has the same striking green eyes as his daughter.

He gazes at me, puzzled. We are sitting around a bamboo patio set in his garden, drinking peach-flavoured ice tea.

'And she wants to make sure you are going to be alright without her,' I continue. 'She further said that it was not your fault that she died. She was just tired of life, yet she loved you so much. She told me you were the best dad in the world and I believe it.'

Haley's dad leans forward in his chair. 'How do you know all these things?'

'She came to me in a vision,' I explain. 'Not a dream, a vivid vision, as if she were alive again. Please, you have to believe me, sir. This is really important to your daughter. She needs peace of mind.'

'I am not sure why you came to me,' he says, 'or what you are gaining from this. But thank you, I appreciate it. She really was such an amazing kid.'

I thought he would be mad at me, but he is clearly not. 'I'm not gaining anything, sir,' I reply. 'She saved my life, so I owe her many favours. This is just one of them.'

Taking the last sip of ice tea, I rise to my feet and thank him for the refreshing drink before saying goodbye.

'Where are you off to now?' Haley's dad asks.

'I want to visit one more place today,' I say, smiling at him. 'I promised Haley that I will rekindle my relationship with my grandad. She made me realise that it shouldn't always be the adults reaching out to the teenagers.'

'Well, I hope everything goes well,' he says, shaking my hand. 'And thank you again.'

'You're welcome, sir. I'm glad I could relay her message.'

***

I arrive at the front door of my grandad's house forty minutes later and knock with a steady hand.

When he answers the door he is grumpy at first. I know why. He likes to take a two-hour nap every afternoon and I am now denying him that little pleasure. I don't care. Patching things up with him is more important than a nap.

'Tom,' is the first word that escapes his mouth. Then his mood lightens and he asks, 'How are you doing, son?'

'Better thank you, Grandpa. I was wondering if I could come in for a while?' I'm surprised to find that it's the first time I'm not feeling scared or anxious around him.

'Yes, of course,' he replies, making a welcome gesture with his hands. He actually appears to be more nervous than I am.

We sit down opposite each other in the dusty lounge and then I say, 'I know we haven't spoken much in the past, but I really want to make an effort to find something we both love, Grandpa. I realised while I was unconscious in the hospital that I've always been a bit unapproachable in my nature. I'm sorry for that.'

'It goes both ways,' he replies, fiddling with his large ears. 'I also should have tried harder and for that I am sorry.'

I stand up and clasp my hands together. 'How about I make us some coffee?'

'That will be nice, Tom. Black with one sugar, please.' He also gets to his feet and adds, 'Let me help you. We can drink our coffee in the kitchen. These couches make me sneeze. I should get them vacuumed some time.'

While drinking coffee and eating ginger bread, we speak for hours. He tells me about his time in the Vietnam war and the friends he made there. I tell him about video games and why I like them so much. We find out that we both love eighties music and we talk about our favourite artists from that era. It is nice to hear him laugh, genuinely laugh, and as the day draws to a close, his smile grows. Because he is finally connecting with his grandson.

Haley was right. I can change things when I'm alive.

I'm not better off dead and my friends and family need me around them. I now inspire them.

I am so unbelievably thankful that Haley, the girl in white, saved my life.